FLIGHT FROM
FIESTA

FLIGHT FROM FIESTA

by

FRANK WATERS

SWALLOW PRESS/
OHIO UNIVERSITY PRESS
ATHENS

Second printing July, 1987.

Originally published as a signed and letterpress edition by The Rydal Press, Santa Fe, 1986.
Swallow Press edition published 1987.
Swallow Press books are published by Ohio University Press.

Library of Congress Cataloging-in-Publication Data

Waters, Frank, 1902–
  Flight from fiesta.

  I. Title.
PS3545.A82F5   1987   813'.52   86–23839
ISBN 0–8040–0891–4
ISBN 0–8040–0892–2 (pbk.)

to

LOLLY

&

BLANDY

From time immemorial they have stood there proud and regally cloaked in pine and piñon, dark blue against the turquoise sky until sunset when they take on the blood-color of their name: the Sangre de Cristo.

Only for three centuries or more has the little, holy city of sun-dried adobe clustered at their foot. But a city proud and regal as its own name: *La Villa Real de San Francisco de la Santa Fe*. Through it have swarmed three races—Indian, Spanish and Anglo—making it in turn the focal center of an ancient and indigenous culture, the outpost capital of the Province of New Mexico, and the oldest capital in the United States.

All this imposing past is at once implicitly and explicitly affirmed each year, on an Indian Summer day, by the simple, mellow chiming of church bells. They are the bells of Saint Francis Cathedral pealing the triumphant news of the reoccupation of the ancient, royal city of the Holy Faith by Don Diego de Vargas and his *conquistadores* in 1692.

To a humble piñon-gatherer on the high slope of the mountains the sound is no different than it ever was. It is still muted by the vast distances that roll and break against him with thunderous silence from the lower foothills, the black volcanic *bajadas* and *picachos*, and the great pelagic plain billowing in from the flat-topped mesas on the western horizon.

Down in town, strangely enough, you can hardly hear the bells for the racket of Fiesta: the honking of automobile horns, the squawk of phonographs, the blare of radios and loudspeakers, the clatter of a marimba. The whole Plaza is an inferno of noise and

[1]

color. Flags and pennants and paper streamers wave from all store fronts. All three races crowd the central park. Blanketed Indians with loads of pottery from a half-dozen pueblos. Spanish *gente de razón* in silver-buttoned vests and tight-fitting *charro* trousers, embroidered shawls and lace mantillas yellowed with age; or *paisanos* in begrimed blue work shirts and black rebozos. Anglo townspeople in Levi's and fancy cowboy boots. Tourists in costume, businessmen sweating in collars and ties. All waiting for De Vargas and his caballeros to ride by in false mustaches, tin helmets and breastplates, on spavined broomtails.

The Reconquest long has lost its historical meaning. For the Spaniards who conquered the Indians have been defeated by the Anglos, and they in turn have fallen victims to the monstrous, mechanistic and materialistic *Máquina* of Progress. It and all its progeny have guts of iron, voices of brass, souls of steel. The *máquinas* rolling in over the paved highways and jamming the parking lots. The *máquinas* blaring out music from the shop windows and blasting out announcements from the rooftops. *Máquinas* pecking out the letters that used to be written in flourishing script by professional scribes; printing newspapers; telling time; planting and harvesting crops; grinding wheat and corn; mixing bread. Mother of God! Nowadays there are even *tortillas de máquina* instead of the *tortillas de la mano* traditionally beaten out only by hand.

Yet one somehow knows even during Santa Fe Fiesta, on an Indian Summer day in old New Mexico, midway through the Twentieth Century, that the immemorial conquest of the spirit by the flesh has still to be achieved. None of the tri-racial conflicts has been settled by the Sword and the Cross, nor by the Great Persuader, Mr. Colt, and the creed of the Almighty Dollar; they have simply gone underground, into the bloodstream. Deep in the hearts of men there still lies hidden a province that not yet has been industrialized by the *Máquina* of Progress.

But now they come! *Saludes, Caballeros!*
Viva La Entrada!
Viva Fiesta!

To the small girl who stood in the forefront of the crowd in the Plaza, the incoming parade offered no diversion of merit. Elsie was some ten years old, dressed in a white frock of imported batiste and patent leather slippers, with pink bobby socks to match the pink ribbons tying her brown pigtails. She stood there stiffly arrogant, her sharp eyes and thin little mouth fitting perfectly into a childish expression of supercilious disdain.

The parade rolled past. Mounted caballeros, marching *soldados*, old ox-carts and *carretas* with wooden wheels, surreys and buckboards. A dirty little *chamaco* in overalls could leap up from the gutter in front of her to hail with joy the sight of his old *primo* riding by on a caparisoned nag. A ragged, sad-eyed girl beside her could jump up and down on bare feet, clapping her calloused brown hands with the wonder and delight of it all. But they were merely children with the prerogatives of ignorance and innocence. The small Anglo *turista* was cut from finer cloth. Elsie's whole appearance labeled her as one of those sophisticated little monsters who already had seen everything, knew everything, and cared about nothing.

In the procession walked an old, white-headed, hawk-faced man with an embittered expression. He was wearing a blood-stained, buckskin jacket, carrying a rifle, and holding in leash a pack of hounds. If the very sight of him disgusted Elsie, the sudden baying of the hounds sent a shiver up her spine. Without waiting for the beribboned float that carried the Fiesta Queen, she threw up her head and skipped across the Plaza.

"Hot dogs! Hamburgers! Lots of mustard!"
"Ice cream cones! Popsicles! Ten cents!"

[3]

Elsie derisively passed the vendors shouting from their booths on each side.

"Tacos, *niña*! *Qué buenos*! They good!"

She paused at the stand just long enough to peek across the greasy linoleum counter at the hot, fried tortillas being packed with meat, onions and lettuce. "They smell!" she said contemptuously in a childish but modulated voice; and pinching her nose with her fingers, skipped away.

Before her stood *El Palacio Real*, a squat and massive adobe extending along the entire north side of the Plaza. She halted a moment at the near corner in front of a bronze plaque on the wall. This Royal Palace of the Governors was the oldest capitol building in the country, the inscription read; for more than three centuries it had housed a hundred governors and captain-generals. Unimpressed as any child, Elsie continued along the wide, open portal whose high roof was upheld by a row of great pillars, each of which had cost the life of a tall pine.

There was no skipping now. The portal swarmed with people looking at the Indians squatting on the brick floor with displays spread out before them. Santa Clara women with black pottery. Tesuque women showing bright-colored little clay animals. San Ildefonso potters offering polished earthen bowls. Taciturn craftsmen who had brought up from Santo Domingo their own flowered ware, and from Cochiti their famous, resonant drums. There were arrays of Zuni and Navajo silver and turquoise jewelry, strings of colored Indian corn, necklaces of squash seeds, Hopi butterfly-yellow pottery and carven kachinas, moccasins, beadwork, trinkets, junk . . . Indians from a dozen different pueblos and tribes who had squatted here through summer heat and winter cold for so many generations that they had become known simply and jocularly as the "Portal Tribe."

Toward the far end of the portal Elsie swerved aside to avoid a man sticking out for her inspection a souvenir bow and several gaudily painted arrows, and bumped forcefully into his wife standing behind him with a sleeping baby wrapped in the shoulder folds of her blanket. The baby, awakened by the jolt, let out a frightened wail. Unconcerned, Elsie merely looked back as she hurried past . . . Only to trip suddenly over a vendor's outstretched legs and fall sprawling on the brick pavement.

Instantly she leapt up, her face distorted by a rage frightening to see in such a small child, and began kicking the pottery vendor's array of small clay animals to shatter against the wall. "You stuck your legs out on purpose! You lazy old Indian! You tripped me!" Jumping up and down now with uncontrollable anger on a few pottery bowls, she finished destroying the whole display. Then fury spent, she stepped back to confront him.

He was a big Pueblo Indian perhaps sixty years old, with a dark, wrinkled face, sitting with his back to the wall. His long hair braids hung down over his broad shoulders, wrapped in a faded red blanket. His long legs still stuck out, clad in ragged pants from which protruded his sloppy moccasins. He continued to sit there without drawing back his offending feet, looking up at her calmly with black, fathomless eyes.

There was something strange and frightening about his dark, impassive face. It showed no resentment, no anger, at what she had done; just a strange and compelling immobility. Elsie drew back and, poised to flee, kicked lightly with one slipper at his outstretched feet.

"It was your fault! You were in my way!"

The old Indian did not move. Nor did his impassive face show any expression as he answered in a soft, deep voice. "Indian here first."

"What are you going to do about it then?" she taunted him, more boldly now, kicking a fragment of broken pottery toward him.

"Indian make. White people break. *Cómo no*? That the way it is." His voice was soft, flat, resigned. But his black eyes kept boring into her.

The little girl's face betrayed a trace of fear and guilt. She squirmed round the portal post, watching the old Indian tenderly gather up the broken fragments of a small clay deer with one dark, wrinkled hand.

"Killin' all them animals. Ai. Ai. Ai. When has it been different?"

Elsie kept waiting for him to jump up and pursue her, to make her pay for his loss, to do something. She was infuriated because he did not.

"Yes I did! I broke 'em all! Everything! Now who's going to pay for 'em?"

The old Indian stealthily reached under his blanket, pulled out a pint flask of whiskey. Taking a hearty swig, he put the bottle back before answering. "White girl pay."

The little girl let out a shriek of laughter. "You're a dirty, drunken old Indian! Drunk! Drunk! That's why you can't do anything! Because you're drunk!"

"White girl pay. I say," the old man answered calmly.

"White girl pay! YOU say!" With a last malicious gibe, Elsie jerked away from the post and ran hurriedly out across the Plaza toward La Fonda Hotel.

It was the cocktail hour in La Fonda. But then every hour was, especially during Fiesta. For if *El Palacio* was the end of all Indian trails from the pueblos and the meeting place for all Spanish neighbors, La Fonda always had been the end of the Santa Fe Trail for Anglo visitors. Pueblo style, the immense and modernized old inn still lived up to its name. The big lobby, cantina, coffee shop and dining room, the patio and inner court all swarmed with townspeople and tourists, most of them in costume.

The Evanses kept waiting patiently for an elevator. Margaret wore a voluminous blue squaw skirt and sherry velveteen blouse, with her chestnut hair tied into a Navajo-style chignon with a purple velvet ribbon. Her husband Tom, a solidly built man with a kindly smile, had come from his law office in a business suit.

"Mrs. Honey Wilbur must be rich as Croesus to afford a whole suite with a private balcony to boot!" she muttered. "Is she as rich as a Texan, Tom?"

"Shhh," he murmured as two pallid and paunchy men in spotless ten-gallon Stetsons strutted by. Then with a whimsical smile he added, "Who is?"

"You say she has a child, a maid, and a Mr. Dixon with her. Who's he? Are they . . ."

"That is none of our business," he said kindly but firmly. "We're not moving in with them, you know . . . Come on. Let's go!"

They went upstairs and Mrs. Honey Wilbur let them in herself. It was a handsome big sitting room, and the sunlight streaming through the balcony windows poured still more honey on her honeyed hair and brought out the creamy tone of the white lace mantilla flung over her shoulders. A strikingly beautiful woman.

"How nice of you to come, Margaret. And what a stunning costume!" she exclaimed, grasping both of Margaret's hands. "Did your husband tell you I went to him to clear my passport into New Mexico?"

Evans grinned. "I know this is still a foreign country to a lot of folks, but I wouldn't exaggerate that much the slight service I was able to do for you, Mrs. Wilbur!"

Honey had a lovely, full-throated laugh. "Well, come in and meet Freddie. I was just mixing us a martini. Or would you like something else?"

Freddie Dixon was slimly built, with a sharp, thin face and an air of quiet elegance. Evans sat down on the end of the couch near his chair. Despite his usual faculty for projecting a new acquaintance against his normal background, he was unable to place Dixon.

[7]

"Your first trip to New Mexico, Mr. Dixon?" he asked pleasantly.

"I've never been Out West before," admitted Dixon. "I really haven't been home at all for several years. You see, I stayed abroad after the war." He deftly flipped open his cigarette case and held it out with a patronizing gesture in which the older man yet detected a faint subservient desire to please.

"No thanks. I gave up those coffin nails some time ago . . . An interesting experience. Is there any hope of solving the political situation in France, do you think?"

Dixon threw up his hand gracefully. "Not politics, please! I never followed them really, you know. There were so many new trends in art and literature to engross one."

Evans nodded approvingly. "I wish I had more time for such things, myself. There's a lot of artists around here whose work might interest you. Margaret will have to take you and Mrs. Wilbur around." Suddenly aware of his hostess' voice, he stopped and turned around.

Honey Wilbur was prattling in a light, sophisticated manner about her small daughter. "Yes, that's my Elsie. A cold and slippery little piece of ice. An incorrigible child, really! Sometimes I wonder where she ever came from . . . Not that I have the slightest idea where she's going!"

Margaret laughed reassuringly. "Now, Honey! I know she must be a little dear. All she needs is to be put into a good school for girls for awhile." She lifted a glass from the tray Honey held out to her and took a tentative sip.

Honey remained standing before her. "Don't be silly, Margaret . . . Is that dry enough for you? Sure? . . . Before Richard and I were divorced, we enrolled her in one school after another. But she kept melting right away. What's the name of that very exclusive one near Boston? Alden's. That's it! Elsie hadn't been there a month before she sneaked into town in a delivery van. Marched right up to the Travelers Aid desk in the railroad station and demanded that Richard be wired to send her transportation home. Of course he did. Richard always spoiled her."

Evans chuckled as he took his glass. "Smart girl!"

"Too smart, Mr. Evans!" answered Honey. "She's willful and selfish, and far too aggressive for her age. After the divorce when I went to Europe, I left her in that nice convent school in Paris while Freddie and I ran down to Seville, and . . ."

"I knew that mantilla came from Spain!" interrupted Margaret. "It's simply gorgeous, Honey. Just wait till you appear at the Ball tonight!"

"Freddie picked it out." Honey smiled warmly and intimately at Dixon, and continued, "I simply don't know what I would have done without Freddie here. There's no place on the Continent he doesn't know. Not only the most charming spots, but actually where one can find a warm room in London! But of course we'd no sooner arrived in Granada than a wire arrived from the Mother Superior of Elsie's convent school in Paris. My little chunk of ice had melted out of her hands, too."

A look of annoyance crept into Dixon's face. Honey noticed it and cut her story short. "We found her in a bistro where she had made friends with the Algerian chef." She turned around inquiringly as a maid entered with a tray of hors d'oeuvres.

"Is Elsie here, Mary?"

"No Ma'am." The maid passed round the tray and set it down.

"I thought I told you to ask Elsie to stay in her room until my guests arrived. They want to meet her."

The maid shrugged helplessly. "I'll tell her if she comes in, Ma'am."

"You see?" said Honey when the maid had gone out, frustration showing through her light, sophisticated manner. "No one has any control of her at all. I often think the child hates people, the way she delights in antagonizing everybody."

"Perhaps that's natural, Mrs. Wilbur," said Evans quietly. "A divorce in the family and lack of the security that only home life can give is often upsetting to a child. Perhaps when you get settled down again things will work out. Don't you think so?"

"But how can I settle down until I figure out what to do with Elsie? I just can't have her following me everywhere, and at the most inopportune times, too. Oh, I sometimes think she ought to be put where she'll really *stay* put, as Freddie recommends . . . But of course she can't. After all, she's my daughter, isn't she?"

Dixon frowned slightly. "Yes, it's a real problem for us both."

Neither of the Evanses answered. The dilemma being forced upon Honey and her lover was obvious to them both.

In the awkward silence Honey strolled over to the balcony window and looked out anxiously. "Oh, I just won't have her ruining Santa Fe for me, too!" she wailed, turning around. "Is this a Fiesta party or a discussion of juvenile delinquency? Freddie, you mix this round! I just can't cope with all these bottle openers, ice shavers, gadgets and all!"

Dixon rose, and as he strolled past her to the buffet-bar, put his hand possessively on her hip. Honey looked out the window again at the swarming Plaza below. "This is gayer than gay Seville! Do you know there's a Santa Fe in Spain, Margaret? Just outside Granada. Remember it, Freddie?"

Dixon smiled, stirring the cocktail shaker gently with a practiced hand and filling the glasses.

Evans spoke up quietly. "Yes indeed, Mrs. Wilbur. And a famous Santa Fe it is, too. It was there King Ferdinand and Queen Isabella received the surrender of the infidel Moors, giving back Spain to Christendom. An obscure fellow named Christopher Columbus was present at the ceremony, if I remember rightly."

Margaret took her glass from Dixon. "That history stuff's too dry, Tom! This is the Santa Fe to be interested in, Honey! Tonight when it gets dark, Zozobra's going to be burned at the stake. Up there on the hill where old Fort Marcy used to stand. He's the huge gargoyle effigy of Old Man Gloom, and his burning starts our Santa Fe Fiesta. Away with gloom! Here's to all us infidels!"

Just as she raised her glass the hall door clicked open. All four turned around to see Elsie standing in the doorway with a supercilious look on her face.

"Tight already?" she asked impertinently.

"Elsie!" exclaimed her mother; and then trying to cover up her embarrassment, "Come in and meet Mother's guests. No more of your little jokes now."

Elsie sauntered in to suffer the introductions. "This is Mrs. Evans . . . Mr. Evans . . . And our Freddie of course, dear!" Elsie swerved suddenly aside, coldly ignoring Dixon.

Only Evans had the kind instinct to move over on the couch. "Won't you sit by me, Elsie?"

Elsie instead walked gracefully over to the bar, sniffed at a couple of the liquor bottles with the curiosity of any child, and then deliberately sauntered back toward the door.

"Elsie!"

The girl stopped and looked back at her mother.

"Mother's going out to dinner and then to the Ball, and will probably be home very late. Mary will give you your dinner and put you to bed. I want you to be a good girl now."

"No need to show off, Mother. That's the way it always is. I'm left out as usual." She turned to a small table set against the wall, and flipped some bills out of her mother's white satin purse.

"Elsie!" screamed Honey indignantly.

"You won't need these few dollars tonight, Mother. Let Freddie pay for a change." With a guileless smile, Elsie stuffed the bills into her own little purse and switched out the door.

Dixon gave a French shrug of helplessness and rose to mix another drink.

[11]

It was sunset when Elsie came out of La Fonda into the Plaza again, creeping stealthily down the street toward the *Palacio Real*. She had lost her swagger and acted like an innocent and imaginative child playing Indian. She stopped and crouched behind a lamp post, oblivious of passers-by. Suddenly she darted across the sidewalk into a shop entrance. Here, hidden behind the dress dummies in the show window, she peeped out toward the portal of the Palace with a strange tenseness in her face and body. Then again she scurried out.

Slowly, one lamp post, one doorway after another, she crept forward. There was a hesitancy about her now, a growing reluctance. She was no longer an eager animal of prey stalking her victim. She herself was the victim. Of what? Curiosity? Fear? Conscience? Whatever it was, it kept dragging her forward against her will. Near the corner she stopped.

The old Indian was still there, outstretched on the portal. He had not bothered to clean up all the litter of his broken pottery. He had, however, summoned the effort to empty the flask of bourbon; Elsie could see the bottle showing under the edge of his blanket. The other vendors were all busy. One of them was packing up his wares. Others were bedding down for the night in order to maintain their places. An Indian woman, finishing suckling her baby, took it from her breast and laid it aside, covering it with her blanket. Then squatting down in front of a charcoal brazier, she began to warm up some tortillas. The smell aroused the old Indian from his nap. He raised his head and sniffed at the air. Then reluctantly he got to his knees and began to gather up his few belongings. As he did so, the empty bottle fell clattering on the brick flooring.

Elsie's face hardened. Regaining her aggressive swagger, she walked across the street.

"White girl pay. Drunk Indian say!" she said mockingly, staring down at him.

The old man looked up at her complacently. Then he got to his feet, flipped his blanket over his head, and walked away. Elsie watched him round the corner with a look of disappointment and surprise. Suddenly compressing her thin lips, she started forward after him.

The old Indian, wrapped in his faded red blanket, plodded steadily up the street as if unaware that the little girl was stealthily following him. In a piece of pasture on the outskirts of town he untethered a bony old mare and hitched her to a rattletrap wagon. Elsie watched him climb unconcernedly onto the plank seat, flip out the reins. "*Ándale! Ándale!*" The old wagon squeaked slowly past her, turned out into the road.

Abruptly and swiftly, Elsie darted after it and climbed into the empty box. The old Indian on the plank seat did not look back. He simply lashed out with the loose reins at the red, sinking sun and in a soft insistent voice shouted again, "*Ándale! Ándale!*"

It was dark when the wagon turned off the highway upon a side road and stopped in front of a drab Mexican lunch counter through whose greasy window pane glowed a kerosene lamp. In its faint aura the old Indian got down from his plank seat and walked inside.

Hesitantly, Elsie followed him. He was sitting on a stool at the empty end of the stained linoleum counter, and did not turn around when Elsie shyly perched on the stool beside him. The *lonchería* was run by a fat and dark Mexican woman, Maria, who was dishing up chiles and beans to two native workmen down at the other end of the counter. One of them wore a dirty shirt and Levi's. The other was dressed in overalls. The kerosene lamp was smoking. The hot stove smelled of grease. It was all so workaday and starkly realistic, contrasting so violently with the playtime Fiesta back in town, that Elsie felt subdued and out of place.

Maria ambled up without greeting, watching the old Indian dig under his blanket into a pocket of his ragged trousers to bring out a nickel which he laid down quietly on the counter. She drew a mug of coffee to set down before him.

The old man's dark, wrinkled hands curved gently around it. It was like a little pot of warm brown earth, and from it he watched grow a little stalk of gray steam. Maria, hands on hips, stood watching him with a scowl on her dark, greasy face. And watching them both with sharp, quick eyes sat Elsie.

"Inocencio!" the woman blurted out at last. "Your belly is hungry and you have no money . . . As usual. And you are too stubborn to say so . . . As usual. No?"

"*Cómo no?*" His soft voice was unconcerned. He was watching the little gray stalk breaking into leaf before him.

Impatiently Maria switched around, heaped a plate with green chiles and beans, and slapped it down in front of him. "So I must feed you . . . As usual! *Pues.* Where is the money from your *primo's* pottery? Those rich *turistas* at Fiesta. They bought it all, no doubt. But now you have no money left to take home. Because you are drunk again. *Borracho! Borracho!*"

Inocencio ignored her. He tore off a piece of leathery tortilla, scooped up some beans, and settled down to eat. Maria turned to the well-dressed little girl sitting watchfully beside him. A quick look passed between them. But it was to the old Indian that she angrily fired another barrage of questions.

"And this *niña* here, Inocencio! This little *turista* child. Who is she? What is she doing with an old drunken Indian when night has fallen? She came in with you. You brought her here! *Verdad!* And yet you eat and leave her hungry! Mother of God!"

She flung around, dished up another plate for Elsie, and poured her a glass of milk. "This Inocencio here," she informed the girl indignantly. "He is no good. He lost his land in the pueblo because he was too lazy to make love. He is not a man at all! How can one be a man without land to work, without a woman to love and beat, without children to work for? No, *niña!*" Her voice kept rising. "He is just a drunk old Indian to whom an ancient mother and widowed sister trust their pottery to sell in town. Do not trust him to take you anywhere. I smell evil in it!"

She waited for the girl to answer. Then she leaned over the counter toward Elsie, pinching her own broad nose with her fingers and shouting, "Do you hear me? I smell the smell of evil in it! Go home to those rich *turistas* where you belong!"

Balked by the noncommittal look in the girl's eyes, she waddled back down to the other end of the counter. She and the two workmen began to mutter indistinctly in Spanish, looking accusingly up the aisle.

Elsie fastidiously wiped off her greasy fork, took a mouthful of hot beans. She prodded among the green chiles for a speck of meat, finally tasted the chiles themselves, and hastily reached for her glass of milk. She still continued to stare at Inocencio eating hungrily in the yellow glow of the smoking lamp. He was a drunken, shiftless old Indian. He had permitted her to destroy his pottery without retaliation. He had allowed Maria to berate him without protest. He was disliked and censured as much by his people as Elsie was by her own people. He had none of the initiative, aggressiveness and self-protection of all the white people Elsie had known . . . And yet there was something about him that refuted all this with a monstrous power and a massive dignity. Without lifting a finger he somehow had drawn her to follow him. Without a word he had compelled Maria, out of her warm peasant kindness, to feed him.

Elsie shivered slightly and took another mouthful of hot beans. There was something strange about this old Indian that she had never encountered. She felt uneasy and frightened of him as she never had been of her mother, Freddie, and all her school authorities. And at the same time she felt a strange sense of security sitting beside him . . . And all this showed in the absorbing stare of her wide eyes on his tall blanketed figure and dark wrinkled face—a childish look at once admiring and distrustful, and above all one of helpless fascination.

Inocencio continued to ignore her. He shoveled the last spoonful of beans into his mouth, drained the coffee mug. He drew his greasy fingers down his long hairbraids, and with quiet dignity wrapped the blanket about his shoulders. For a moment he sat in full content. Then he stood up facing Maria, and raising thumb and forefinger to his throat made the old Indian sign of repletion —of a belly too full for more.

"*Gracias, mi amiga!*" A beautiful smile illumined his dark, impassive face, revealing a facet of his character that Elsie had not seen before. Without a look at her, he strode out the door.

"Good!" said Maria, coming up to the girl. "Now, *mi niña*, this *compadre* here has a pickup truck." She nodded toward one of the workmen. "He will drive you where you belong. No doubt your family, those *ricas*, will reward him well for returning a lost child. What did you say your name was, *niña*?"

Elsie looked at her without answering, and then at the workman paying his bill. Abruptly she jumped off her stool and bolted out the door. The old Studebaker wagon was slowly drawing out of the faint aura of light into the darkness. She reached it just as it turned into the road, and again clambered into the box behind Inocencio.

The moon was coming up when the wagon drew into the cluttered courtyard of an Indian summer home on the outskirts of the pueblo. Its greenish-gray light outlined the shapes and shadows of two small adobes squatting near a clump of great cottonwoods, an

[16]

anthill adobe oven, a drying rack from which hung a fresh sheep pelt, and a log corral. Inocencio got down and began to unhitch the mare.

At the clatter of the singletree, the door of one of the adobes opened. The oblong light streaming past the shadow of a woman standing in the doorway revealed Inocencio unharnessing. It also lit up Elsie's white dress as she clambered out of the box and stood watching him. Inocencio gave the mare a swat on the rump to send her into the corral, closed the gate after her. Then walking past Elsie without a glance, he entered the adobe and closed the door behind him.

As Elsie stood in the darkness, a little greenish-gray ghost without will or power to move, the door was suddenly flung open again and the silhouetted woman impatiently beckoned.

The house Elsie entered was a single big room with a hard-packed dirt floor and clay-whitened walls on which were hung only a few calendar saints. In the far corner was an iron bedstead, and beside it a worn saddle. Inocencio was sitting in front of a small, conical fireplace in the other corner. Squatting against the wall on a sheepskin in front of a litter of freshly fired pottery was his mother, an old withered crone with rheumy eyes, straggly hair, and hands like the prehensile talons of a hawk. As Elsie hesitated, the woman who had let her in motioned her to the chair at the table in the middle of the room. On it was set a kerosene lamp.

The woman was Inocencio's widowed sister, middle-aged and heavy-set, with a sad but beautiful face, and dressed in a wrinkled, flowered print held around the waist by a wide, embroidered Hopi sash. When the girl sat meekly down, she walked toward Inocencio with a stern but calm face. Her moccasins made no sound.

"You return from Fiesta but you bring back none of our pots."

"You say it, Pilar," assented Inocencio.

"Then you bring us some dollars for our work?"

"No dollars," said Inocencio gravely.

[17]

Pilar hitched up her belt, stepped closer to him, stooped and smelled his breath. "Do I smell that whiskey again?"

"I drank. But not much. A little bottle. Just enough to ease my weakness," he answered with assured candor.

Pilar drew back. "No pots. No dollars. No whiskey . . . No, you are not drunk like many times. So I ask where are those pots, them little animals we gave you to sell for us?"

Inocencio turned his dark, somber face to look around the room. His black eyes grew blacker. "Indian make. White people break. When has it been different?"

The little girl squirmed on her chair in the middle of the room. She was still curiously and outwardly ignored, an experience new to her. Yet at the same time she felt the effect of her presence upon them all: their heavy, silent, Indian negation of her kind, the growing tension in the air. It was all so strange and Indian, strong and subdued. It had none of Maria's Spanish emotionalism, none of her mother's nervous excitability. Unable to stand it, she jumped up aggressively.

"I want a drink of water!" she demanded petulantly and arrogantly in her childish voice.

None of them looked at her. Pilar merely nodded toward a bucket of water on a bench against the wall. Elsie, put in her place without a word, went over and dipped out a drink.

Pilar's voice began again, but in a sharper tone. "I killed our last sheep while you were loafing at Fiesta. I slit his throat, I skinned, I butchered—I, a woman! But we have no salt for our meat. There is some coffee but no sugar. The store will give us no more flour. Brother, where are the dollars for them pots we gave you? Who will pay for them?"

"She pay," Inocencio said doggedly in a soft voice. "That White one who broke them."

Elsie raised to her knees on the chair. "It was his fault! He was drunk! I saw him!" she shouted childishly.

[18]

Inocencio did not look at her, nor did Pilar turn around. They still ignored her, as Indians ignore a child while discussing serious matters. But suddenly the old, withered crone let out a low, keening cry. Struggling to her skinny legs, she hobbled across the room to loose upon Inocencio a torrent of invective. It was in their own *idioma*; she could not speak English, and seldom spoke Spanish.

"Are you a man?" Pilar's shrill voice repeated her mother's accusations. "Our mother has seen you lose your land. She has heard the Council judge you because you will not do your pueblo duties. So you come here for two women to feed you. Do you bring a wife and sons to help us? Do you do the work of my man who was killed? Pagh! You are not a man! You are a pig! It would be better if we put you out!"

She strode across the floor, grabbed up the old worn saddle, and heaved it out the door. "Go!" she shouted. "We can stand no more!"

Elsie, standing by the water bucket, heard Pilar's accusations echo those of Maria. They confirmed her own resentment. Yet she felt disturbed. She put down the dipper and slid quietly back to her chair at the table.

Inocencio calmly stirred the coals in the fireplace. "Can I quarrel with women?" he asked himself loudly. Then stretching out his hand behind him, "Mother, hand me that coffee pot!"

The old woman thrust the blackened pot at him and hobbled back to her sheepskin. Inocencio set the pot on the red coals and ignoring Pilar's stare, waited for it to warm. After a time he poured a trickle of coffee into a tin cup and took a sip.

"Now! We will talk!" shouted Pilar. "About this White girl!"

"What White girl?" Inocencio asked innocently.

"This one! Here! You brought her! Why?"

Inocencio looked blandly at Elsie as if seeing her for the first time, then turned to Pilar. "You saw me get out of my wagon.

You saw me come in the house and close the door. Was it not you who opened it and called this one in from the darkness? Why?"

"*Maldito!*" shrieked Pilar. "Who is she? Where does she come from? Why is she here? To bring the policemens upon us poor Indians?"

Inocencio swallowed the dregs of the coffee pot and asked complacently, "Who knows? She is little and wears a white dress like an Angel from the White people's Heaven. Mebbe she come to pay two poor Indian women for them broken pots."

"I won't! I won't!" Elsie shouted childishly.

Inocencio stood up, flipping his blanket over his shoulder with the habitual and immemorial gesture of his people. "Too much talkin'. I go sleep now." Without more ado he strode out the door.

An uneasy look flitted across Elsie's face. She jumped down and ran after him to the door. The old Indian, without a backward look, walked into the adjacent adobe hut and closed the door. Elsie hesitated, then turned around to find Pilar confronting her.

"So! You have no name! You are runnin' away! You have come to bring policemens upon us!"

Elsie, with the instant adaptability of children, regained her assurance. She sauntered over to kneel in front of the old crone and her litter of pottery. An array of little clay animals caught her fancy. How beautiful they were! So finely molded, so brightly colored, so naively alive! Elsie smiled with childish pleasure.

"A deer! Look, a skunk! And this? I've never seen one!" She held up a small beaver.

The two women, muttering together in the *idioma*, paid no attention to her. Elsie interrupted them by carelessly flipping a bill out of the little satin purse swinging from her arm, and thrusting it at the old woman. "I'll buy 'em all! Here!"

The woman's bony, withered hand avidly reached out to grasp it. Pilar gave a snort. "I don't like it! You get us in trouble sure . . . But we don't put you out in the dark like no dog."

She yanked a blanket off the iron bedstead, and spread it over a serape on the wide seating ledge that extended along the wall. "You sleepin' here!"

Elsie still stood admiring her little clay animals in the light of the flickering lamp.

Honey Wilbur in her bedroom in La Fonda next morning helplessly posed for a perfect portrait of a Fiesta hangover. She lay in bed, her rumpled hair loose on the pillow, trying to hide her face from a peeping lens of early sunlight. Beside the bed lay her collapsed heap of lingerie. Her dejected gown clung to a chair. The stockings and white lace mantilla were strewn on the floor.

At the sound of a loud and prolonged knocking, she rolled over, groaning, and yanked the covers over her head. There was another knock; then Mary, the maid, opened the door a crack and peeked in. "Mrs. Wilbur! It's terribly important! Please, Mrs. Wilbur!"

Honey lifted up with another groan to throw the pillow at her. "Coffee! Not a word before my coffee! Hear!"

The maid ducked back only to reappear almost instantly with a tray which she set on the bed table. She picked up the pillow, helped Honey into her dressing gown, and poured out some coffee. "It's Miss Elsie, Ma'am," she confessed excitedly. "She's gone. It's terrible, Mrs. Wilbur!"

Honey took a gulp of hot coffee. "Oooh! That child again!" Abruptly she sat bolt upright. "Gone? Well, where is she?"

Mary stood twisting her hands. "She didn't come in to breakfast, so I went to her room. It was neat as a pin. Her bed hadn't been slept in . . . Oh, Mrs. Wilbur! I'm scared something's happened to her!"

[21]

"Well, go to the manager. Ask him to check the bellhops, porters, maids, everybody! You'll find her."

The maid ran out. Honey sat holding her head with both hands. "Freddie! FREDDIE!"

"O.K. I hear you!" his voice sounded from the adjoining room.

In a moment the door opened. Dixon stood there in his dressing robe, yawning and running a hand through his rumpled hair. "What's the matter? You must have a head, letting off so much steam so early in the morning."

"Why shouldn't I, after that damned Fiesta Ball?" Honey replied crossly. "I hate champagne! I'd rather drink pure vinegar!"

He grinned. "That's what I thought last night when you insisted on opening the last magnum." He sat down on the bed beside her, lightly and teasingly running his fingers up her bare arm.

Honey jerked it away, twisting her head away from him. "Freddie! No! . . . Elsie's missing! She wasn't in her room all last night."

"Don't worry about it, Honey," Dixon said soothingly. "She'll turn up. She always does." He leaned down, slowly pulled aside the covers, and kissed her on the throat.

Honey stiffened, but only to feel his hand slip under the covers and gently close upon her breast. That was the way it had been from the start. A gentle insistence that had at once a teasing tenderness and an insidious stubbornness that could not be denied. Freddie Dixon had no sharp corners: no overt advances to be repulsed, no decided preferences nor schedules to be rigidly adhered to like Richard's, no dominant opinions to be combatted. He had only this gentle insistence that never forced nor hurried, but which sometimes frightened her by its potency to find and turn the key to her response.

They both heard the quick patter of feet coming down the hall. Even before Mary knocked on the door, Dixon stood up and reached casually for a cigarette.

"Come in, Mary!" called Honey.

[22]

The distressed maid came in talking. "She isn't here, Mrs. Wilbur! The manager had the house detective check everybody. No one's seen Miss Elsie except a bellboy who saw her go out last evening just before six o'clock . . . Oh, Mrs. Wilbur! What'll we do?"

She hastened mechanically to gather up the clothes strewn on floor and chair, and drew the curtains to let in the bright morning sun.

Dixon sank down into a chair at the writing desk with a scowl. "That damned kid again! I hope this time she stays gone!"

Honey jumped out of bed to face him. "I won't have you saying that, Freddie! After all, she's my child. You've got to help me find her."

The maid hurried over to pour a cup of coffee, handing it to him in a conciliatory manner. Dixon stirred it moodily.

"Oh, stop the dramatics, Honey. She's probably picked up a kitchen maid or somebody as usual. Like that Negro chauffeur in London who taught her to drive a car."

Honey walked to the window and nervously peered out. "Elsie doesn't like us or any of our friends, Freddie. Maybe that's why she picks up with such people. What do they give her I don't?"

Dixon took a gulp of coffee, making a grimace of distaste. "This coffee's cold!"

"Get some more, Mary," directed Honey. "Strong and HOT!"

When the embarrassed maid went out, she turned to Dixon. "How COULD you talk to me like that in front of Mary, Freddie?"

"Oh, stop it! She's no fool!"

"Neither am I!" shouted Honey with her first show of spirit. "When you fail to show me a little courtesy in front of my own maid, and have absolutely no concern for the safety of my daughter, I begin to wonder."

The telephone rang. She ran to the bed table to answer it. "Yes, this is Mrs. Wilbur. Oh yes . . . No. I didn't miss her until this morning. You see, I went out with friends to dinner and the Fiesta Ball, and didn't get in until late. Naturally I supposed she was safe at home . . . Yes, I will. Immediately. Thank you."

Honey put the receiver down slowly and turned to Dixon. "That was the manager. He says this might be serious with all the Fiesta crowds in town. He insists we notify the police."

"I'll telephone. Go on and get dressed." Dixon walked over to the telephone and placed his call as Honey went into the dressing room, leaving the door open a crack to listen to his conversation.

"The Police Department? Do you have a Bureau of Missing Persons or something like that? . . . Then I'll talk with the chief."

As he began to talk, Honey stuck her head out the door. "Be sure and tell him we didn't miss her until this morning on account of the Ball! I don't want him to think we just let her run wild without any notice whatever!"

Dixon ignored her and continued talking . . . "Elsie Wilbur . . . Ten, I think. Brown hair, worn in pigtails. White dress. Pink bobby socks, black slippers, a little white purse·. . . Yes? No, I'm not. . . . Frederick J. Dixon . . . I'm a friend of her mother . . . Yes, about six o'clock last night when one of the bellboys . . . yes, suite 315 at La Fonda . . . one of the bellboys saw her leave."

Not yet dressed and with her honey hair still loose, Honey rushed out of the dressing room and grabbed the receiver from him. "A very pretty little girl, too! You'll recognize her the instant you see her . . . What? Of course I'm her mother! Mrs. Honey Wilbur. Naturally there's a reward . . . Yes, I'll bring one right down. Thank you, Chief!"

She put down the receiver, and bending down to set the seam of one stocking straight, smiled hopefully up at Dixon. "He'll find her! I can tell from his voice. He's going to check every Fiesta concession and movie in town, every place a child could go. That's why he wants me to bring him a photo of Elsie. The reward must

[24]

be worthwhile, too. Radio announcements will be made on all newscasts asking anybody who has seen her to let us know."

Dixon shrugged. "Here we go again. When will it ever end?"

In the same bright, early morning sunlight the Indian courtyard looked more tawdry and run-down than in last night's moonlight. But it also looked more peaceful and homey with the old mare munching hay in the corral and birds flitting among the giant cottonwoods along the stream. Inocencio had built a fire in the conical adobe oven and was squatting in front of it, roasting a slab of mutton ribs. His old mother was combing her straggly thin hair nearby, and Elsie was playing with her little clay animals.

They all looked up when Pilar trudged into the courtyard carrying a heavy flour sack. Unslinging it from her broad shoulder, she emptied on the ground before them a litter of groceries she had brought from the trading post at the pueblo: salt, sugar, coffee, a small sack of flour, a pot of jam, and some chocolate cookies.

"Ai. Ai. Ai," exclaimed Inocencio. "We got salt for our meat. Sugar for our coffee. Bread and jam to put on him. Ai! Chocolate cookies!" With almost comic haste he flipped over the ribs and settled the coffee pot on the coals. Then he looked blandly at Elsie. "Who buy all them groceries? Mebbe White girl pay. I say."

Elsie jumped up with a petulant frown like a child who suddenly realizes she has been outsmarted by a grownup. "I didn't! I won't!"

Pilar with quiet dignity handed her a big, red lollipop. Elsie grabbed it and began to tear off its paper wrapping before stuffing it into her mouth. "It's the 'Pink Puppy' kind! I like them best!"

In a little while they ate. Inocencio ravenously stripping meat from ribs. Pilar tearing off a chunk of Indian bread and spreading it thick with jam. The old woman pouring a handful of sugar into her coffee, Indian fashion, and slowly sipping the sickeningly sweet mixture with relish. None of them looked at Elsie nibbling on a rib held in one hand, holding her lollipop in the other, and keeping her eyes on the chocolate cookies. There was no Mary here to forbid her indulgence in sweets, no mother to preach of a dietetically balanced meal. With both hands full, she reached out for a cookie and dropped her lollipop on the ground. Stuffing the whole cookie in her mouth, she licked off bits of grass from the sticky sucker with a chocolate-coated tongue, and eyed another cookie.

It was a scene of an Indian family leisurely eating breakfast outside on a sunny morning that carried an atmosphere of charm, simplicity and peacefulness. It was enhanced by the faint ringing of a church bell.

Inocencio finally straightened up with a contented sigh. "Ah, qué bueno!" Elsie watched him wipe his greasy fingers on his long pigtails, and slyly imitated him.

"Meat. Bread. Coffee. Them chocolate cookies." He enumerated his satisfactions. "But no little drink. Not even for Fiesta!"

"No drink," answered Pilar quietly. "You have that little bottle for Fiesta yestiddy."

Inocencio rose and strolled down to the stream that ran beside the big cottonwoods. As they watched his tall body bend down to drink, Pilar said suddenly, "He got that weakness, that man. But he got the power, too!"

The girl looked at her with a curious expression that was not entirely curiosity. "What's that?"

"That something White people don't know nothing!" Pilar looked straight at Elsie. "You feel him here just the same!" She put her hand on her breast.

When Inocencio walked back in the silence, Pilar stood up decisively. "Now you takin' this White girl to that bus!" And turning to Elsie she said sharply, "You go home now. I say it!"

Inocencio stretched lazily. "Mebbe pretty soon. Mebbe see our people dancin' first."

[26]

"We goin' now! I say it!" insisted Pilar.

She and the old woman washed the few dishes and cups in the stream, made ready to leave. In a few minutes they walked slowly out of the courtyard. Inocencio stalking sedately ahead in his faded red blanket. Pilar wearing a gaudy, flowered shawl and a pair of knee-high, white deerskin boots, and staggering under a load of pottery. The old woman in a black rebozo and hobbling along with her stick. And Elsie meandering along behind them, still sucking her red lollipop and carrying her little clay animals in a paper bag.

How beautiful it was, this dusty lane winding through the Reservation in the richness and ripeness of a September morning. The thickets of wild plum and chokecherry on each side were heavy with fruit. Milpas of squaw corn shone pale yellow in the sunlight. Behind clumps of great cottonwoods the mountain slopes rose out of sage and piñon into ridges of spruce and pine. Another summer house and still another appeared—chocolate-mud adobes raised at random from fields and pastures fenced with peeling aspen poles that followed the natural contours of land and stream instead of being squared with the cold precision of surveyors stakes. Perhaps this pueblo Reservation was but an isolated island in a sea of materialistic conformity; yet it still held the beauty and freshness of the pristine wilderness past.

The small group stopped at a crossing where the irrigation ditch had broken and the water was pouring across the road. Inocencio pulled up his blanket, spread his long legs, and nimbly for an old man leaped across it. As Elsie stepped up to imitate him, the old woman jabbered excitedly. Pilar caught the girl, jerked her back. Getting down on her knees, she carefully began wiping off Elsie's wet slipper with her flowered shawl.

"Costin' lots of money, them shiny shoes!" she scolded. "Better bein' more careful!"

Elsie didn't mind the scolding. She rather liked the feeling of

Pilar on her knees industriously scrubbing her wet slipper. It was almost as good as feeling wanted.

Inocencio jumped back, rudely swung her across his hip, and waded back across the stream. Pilar and her mother detoured through the field to join them. They all resumed their slow plodding up the road.

More and more travelers began to catch up and pass them: Indians on foot, all dressed in their best shawls and blankets; Spanish neighbors in wagons and pickups; visitors and tourists in lines of dusty cars. A big sound truck slowly crawled by, its loudspeaker blaring out a radio announcement from Santa Fe:

> In addition to the remaining attractions programmed for the annual Santa Fe Fiesta, a Corn Dance will take place today in Tewa Pueblo. Many visitors to our Land of Enchantment are planning to take this opportunity of seeing for the first time an authentic Indian dance . . .

The road straightened out and the little group stopped in front of the trading post at the entrance to the pueblo. Pilar wearily let down her heavy load and began taking out the pottery from the sack. The old woman squatted down against the wall of the post, spread out a blanket on the ground, and began to neatly arrange the pieces on it. Inocencio unconcernedly strolled off toward the pueblo plaza. For a moment Elsie stood watching him. Then she thrust at Pilar the paper sack containing her little clay animals.

"Don't you sell them! They're mine!" She skipped away to follow Inocencio.

The pueblo suddenly broke upon her with a pageant of life and riotous color. The adobe walls and flat rooftops were already crowded with people, their brilliant shawls and blankets a solid mass of green, pink, blue, cerise, purple, orange and yellow against the farther mountain wall. On the highest rooftop stood a solitary figure wrapped in stainless white, intoning in a high-pitched voice a resonant and monotonous call. He was the cacique making his announcements. In the plaza below, pottery, jewelry and blanket vendors were setting out their wares. A man in overalls was tacking a piece of bunting across the front of a hot dog stand. Dogs and children were running everywhere . . . To Elsie it seemed a strangely real and barbarically colored contrast to the extravagantly make-believe, Spanish-Anglo Fiesta of Santa Fe the day before.

Its strangeness was suddenly intensified by a fantastic figure trotting into the plaza. He was naked save for a black loin cloth, his ash-gray body splotched with blobs of black and earth-brown, his face weirdly painted with zigzag lines. His hair, plastered with white clay, was drawn up into a tuft on top of his head from which stuck up a cluster of dry, brittle corn husks. A human corn cob; a blackened ghost of an old cornstalk. Shaking a twig of spruce, he trotted along in moccasins wrapped in black and white skunk fur.

A naked child playing in the dirt screamed as he approached. A woman dashed out of a doorway, grabbed up the child, and fled back inside. The strange figure stopped, glared round the plaza, then slowly crept toward Elsie.

The girl gave way slowly, looking around with an uneasy glance. Inocencio was walking into the little church. Elsie bolted from the strange figure to follow Inocencio inside.

Mass was over and the big bare room, its nave devoid of pews, benches or chairs, was empty save for Inocencio. Standing quietly inside the doorway, she saw him kneeling humbly on the hard adobe floor in front of the sanctuary. The old altar long had fallen under the condemnation of the visiting padre; there remained of it only a single panel of hand-hewn wood painted with a cornstalk half hidden by the fold of a velvet drape. In the flickering candlelight Elsie could see a rudely carved *bulto* and several *santos* banished to the shadowed walls of the transept. For a long time the old Indian did not move. Nor did Elsie, confronted with an aspect of him she had not suspected.

[29]

Finally Inocencio rose, drawing his blanket about him, and walked slowly back up the nave past Elsie as if he did not see her. Elsie followed him out the door and around the edge of the plaza. Stopping at a booth to buy an ice-cream cone—a double-decker— she watched him pause in front of a group of *compadres* huddling against a wall. One of them furtively handed him a whiskey bottle. Inocencio spread his legs, took a long swallow. The man tried to take the bottle back. Inocencio twisted aside, taking another longer swig before he gravely handed it back. The man held it up to the light, scowling. Inocencio nodded politely and imperturbably, and walked on. In the middle of the plaza he stopped, folding his arms across his chest in a posture of dignified attention.

Elsie, the dwindling lollipop in one hand and the ice cream cone in the other, slowly walked up to stand beside him. "Drunk old Indian!" she taunted him once more.

Inocencio deigned not to notice her. Warm with whiskey, he stared out into the plaza. It was more crowded now, the entrance choked with cars and wagons. There were more fantastic, painted figures now, running around scaring children, making fun of Anglo tourists and Spanish neighbors with ironic mimicry, and shouting derisively at the dignified cacique on the high rooftop. They were the Black Eyes, the *Chiffoneta*, the *Koshares*, the fun-makers, the sacred clowns. Immune to all temporal authority, they even cavorted with mocking pantomime around the Governor who stood clutching his cane of office, one of the little mahogany canes with silver-plated heads presented by Abraham Lincoln to each pueblo in acknowledgment of its right to local sovereignity.

Their antics were interrupted by a curious hush falling over the crowd. Inocencio's broad grin narrowed. Elsie moved closer to him. She could hear it now. It was the soft, deep and resonant beat of a big belly drum. A long line of beautifully garbed and painted figures was filing into the plaza. The dance was about to begin.

Anastasio Cerillos, chief of police, sat behind his desk quietly studying the photograph of Elsie which had been handed him. Honey, sitting with Dixon in front of him, continued talking in a rising voice.

"But she's been missing since last evening, and here it is the middle of the morning and you haven't found her yet! How can a small girl stay lost so long?"

The chief was a big, heavyset man, too old to be stampeded by an indignant tourist, and too Spanish to betray annoyance. He laid down the photo and looked up with a kindly smile.

"Believe me, Mrs. Wilbur," he said suavely, "we're doing everything possible to find your pretty little needle in this haystack of Fiesta visitors. We're checking all amusements, every concession. I'm going to notify the county sheriff, too. She may have strayed out of town."

"What for? Of course not!"

"Now Honey! Don't get upset!" protested Dixon, "Go on back to the hotel in case somebody calls in. I'll go talk to the sheriff myself. The chief here's got his hands full."

Cerillos rose. "The sheriff's office is in the County Court House. It's just a block west of the *Palacio*. I'll keep in touch with him. We work together at all times, you know." He turned to Honey. "Rest assured we'll do the best we can to find your little girl, Mrs. Wilbur."

They shook hands, and Honey and Dixon went out.

"Never trust these small-town officials," said Dixon as they walked down the street toward La Fonda. "I learned that much in Europe."

"But this is the United States, Freddie, even though it doesn't seem like it at times."

"It's Spanish just the same . . . You know what that is. *Mañana, mañana.*"

He left her in front of the hotel on the corner, and hurried across the plaza to the big, Spanish-Colonial County Court House. The county sheriff, Jim Mann, was a tall man with a star pinned to his neat business suit—an Anglo who looked sensible and efficient. He introduced his undersheriff loafing on a chair by the window. Shorty Thompson was a sawed-off, ex-cowpoke wearing a vest, gambler's striped trousers tucked into high-heeled cowboy boots, and a battered Stetson from which protruded a prominent cowlick of unruly brown hair. He did not get up, and went on rolling a stubby cigarette from a sack of Bull Durham and a brown Wheatstone paper. Dixon ignored him, and settled down to business with the sheriff.

"I'm speaking confidentially, sheriff. But I really don't suspect any foul play. The girl is habitually running away from her mother and every school she's enrolled in."

Shorty scratched a match on his boot tip with a flourish and lit his cigarette. "A lil' maverick, hey? Allays cuttin' out from the herd!"

Dixon threw him a look of annoyance. Then turning back to the sheriff, he added a hasty postscript to his remarks. "You understand my position, sheriff. We must not distress Mrs. Wilbur, of course. Yet I feel it my duty to tell you this in order to be of practical assistance."

"A cow's goin' to bawl fer her calf, hell er high water, Mister," drawled Shorty.

"So you think there's a possibility that the child has deliberately run away, Mr. Dixon?" asked the sheriff. "Did she have any money on her at all, do you think?"

Dixon leaned forward and slapped the table with the flat of his hand. "Why didn't I think of it myself? Of course! A few minutes before she left the hotel, the girl took out of her mother's purse a roll of bills. I don't know how much, but it was more than a little."

Shorty's slow drawl broke in again. "So you reckon she's high-tailin' it? Why? Wan't the home pasture green enough fer her, Mister?"

Dixon turned on him angrily. "Please! These irrelevant comments . . ."

The sheriff hastily interrupted. "I've asked Mr. Thompson here, as my undersheriff, to work with the city police and do all he can to find the child. I'll also ask the state police to send out a call to all officers on patrol to keep an eye out for her. We'll keep you and Mrs. Wilbur advised of any developments, of course." He reached for the telephone, clearly a gesture of dismissal.

Dixon got up, and ignoring Shorty walked out the door.

Instead of returning to her hotel rooms, Honey went to Evans' office. When she was finally admitted, she wasted no time in preliminaries.

"Mr. Evans, I'm worried about Elsie. She's been missing since last night. The chief of police is doing all he can to find her. Apparently the county sheriff will, too. But something tells me something about her disappearance is terribly wrong."

"What?"

"How do I know what I know?"

"That's not much to go on, Mrs. Wilbur. Why not start at the beginning?"

"There's no beginning. Richard always spoiled Elsie. He was always too concerned about business to give her any time—or me. So he gave her expensive presents instead, and me too. That's why we were divorced, Richard and I."

"But certainly he loves her, is concerned about her welfare. Do you think we should advise him of her present disappearance?"

"And have him fly out here, turn over the whole state to do no more than is being done now—and endanger my relationship with

Freddie? They've never met, you know." When he did not answer, she continued swiftly. "I met Freddie in Europe where I'd taken Elsie soon after my divorce. We formed a close attachment from the start, and he kept us company during our travels. He is a dealer in antiques, objets d'art, paintings, that sort of thing. But with his increasing sales to the United States, he was thinking of making his home base in this country. So I brought him back with me. We're thinking of getting married if we can find a place suitable for both a home and his business—Santa Fe here, Carmel or Palm Springs in California, some such place. But Elsie is another problem."

"Yes," said Evans.

"Oh, it's natural she and Freddie have never got along. The publicity given my divorce, the shocked amazement of my friends, our uprooting from an established life, our flight to Europe. What a horrible time! Not even with my ample funds could I escape the nagging feeling of being lost and aimless. Only Freddie saved me. But not Elsie. She was always too fond of her father, and resented Freddie from the start. Nor can I blame Freddie. Sensitive as he is, he's always been footloose, without the responsibility of such a wayward child."

"I understand."

Honey took a deep breath, then blurted it out. "But with this disappearance of Elsie, I've begun to wonder if Freddie resents Elsie, if he wants to get rid of her. Not that I blame him, but . . . "

Evans fiddled with the pens and papers on his desk. "Mrs. Wilbur, I'm just a lawyer in a comparatively small town. Not a psychologist. But it seems to me that the cause of Elsie's disappearance is rooted in her insecurity with you and Mr. Dixon. That is your problem."

"No, it isn't!" said Honey forthrightly. "The problem is Elsie's disappearance. She's got to be found! So I've come to ask you to take over the management of the search for her, to coordinate all the efforts of the city police, the sheriff's office, the State Highway Patrol."

"I'll do what I can to help you, Mrs. Wilbur."

The sun stood high in the cloudless sky, beating down with hot brilliance upon the two women squatting against the wall of the trading post. The dance had begun in the plaza of the pueblo. They could hear the deep, steady beat of the big belly drum, the faint clatter of gourd rattles, and the deer-hoof and turtle-shell rattles tied to the legs of the dancers. Traffic had stopped on the road in front of them; the sides of the road and the entrance to the plaza were choked with parked cars. The dust had settled, too, covering the old woman's black rebozo. She patiently shook if off, and wiped off her dry lips with her skinny forearm.

Pilar dutifully dug out from their few belongings a battered tin cup and went into the trading post. The big room, cluttered with merchandise, was empty of customers. The trader stood behind the long counter fussing with a portable radio. He did not look up. Pilar stood holding out her tin cup, and listening to the sputter and static of the little *máquina*. There was a sudden blasting roar. The trader turned it down, gave a last twist to his screwdriver, and adjusted the dial to bring a voice in tune.

"There! That's got her!" He took the tin cup from Pilar and walked to the back to fill it with water.

Pilar remained staring at the *máquina* with an expression of shocked surprise growing into frantic alarm as she listened to the announcer's voice:

... missing since six o'clock last night when she was report-edly seen following an unidentified Indian from the Palace of the Governors. The little lost girl is wearing a white dress, pink hair ribbons and bobby socks, and black patent leather slippers. A substantial reward is offered for information lead-

[35]

ing to her return to her mother. Please notify the Police Department . . .

Without waiting for her cup of water, Pilar threw her shawl over her head and ran out. At the entrance to the pueblo she stopped, looking frantically around the crowded plaza. They were dancing now: a long, straight line stretching in front of the circular chorus of old men, their deep voices soughing like the wind through the pines, and accompanied by the still deeper voice of the big drum. The men, alternating with the women, were painted a golden copper to the waist. Each wore a Hopi ceremonial kirtle, with a fox skin hanging behind, and moccasins trimmed with a band of skunk fur. In the right hand they carried a gourd rattle, in the left a sprig of evergreen.

The drummer flipped up the other end of his big drum. The rhythm changed. The women stepped forth, making two lines now in front of the circle of singing old men. Barefooted, their squat figures were covered by loose, black *mantas* leaving one shoulder free, and belted with embroidered red and green sashes. Each carried on her head a turquoise-blue *tablita*, a thin wooden tiara perhaps a foot high, shaped like a doorway, painted with cloud symbols, and tipped with eagle down. Keeping time with sprigs of evergreen, they wheeled slowly, forming with the men two great circles revolving in front of the drummer with his big drum and the raptly singing chorus.

Now was the time. Before the weaving, dancing *Koshares* could stop her, Pilar ran between the circles to the other side of the plaza. There she saw them standing in the forefront of the crowd, Inocencio stolidly watching and Elsie licking her ice cream cone.

Running up to them, she said tensely in a low voice, "This White girl! Runnin' away! I hear him on that *máquina* in the store! . . . The policemens are comin'! It bad, bad, bad! Just like I say!"

The relaxed, childish look on Elsie's face was replaced immediately by the hard expression of suspicion, resentment and aggressiveness that the old Indian had seen before. "Freddie! That damned Freddie's done this! He said he'd put me in jail or the reform school!"

Only the word "jail" was intelligible to Inocencio and Pilar. They stared at each other aghast with the old, old Indian fear of White authority. Unobtrusively and swiftly they hurried out of the plaza to stop in the now deserted road where the old crone sat dozing against the wall of the trading post. Here they were confronted by the problem of what to do with the little White girl.

"You go!" ordered Pilar quickly and decisively. "Go! You bringin' us poor Indians trouble!"

Elsie, hard and alert now, grabbed up her little paper bag of clay animals to clutch with her lollipop and dwindling ice cream cone. "They won't catch me!" She darted down the road.

Inocencio stood staring after her with a curious expression on his big, dark face. It was his moment of decision. He had ignored her from the start, disclaimed any responsibility for her presence here, and now she was gone. But the same queer feeling that had drawn Elsie to go with him now compelled Inocencio to follow her. Why? The old Indian did not know. He was a little too tight to care. He simply trotted after her.

"We get that wagon. Ridin' better than walkin'," he said, catching up with her.

The girl twisted around, giving him a contemptuous look. "That old slow horse and wagon? You're crazy!"

She walked on, peeking in the cars parked along the side of the road. Abruptly she stopped, seeing a key left in the ignition lock of a dark blue sedan. She jerked the door open, pushed Inocencio into the driver's seat, then ran around the front of the car and got in beside him.

"Go on! Start it!"

The old Indian sat bolt upright in his blanket, completely frozen and befuddled. The girl leaned over him, spilling the ice cream out of her cone upon his lap, and twisted the ignition key. The car was in gear, and jumped back to bang into the bumper of the car behind. Inocencio reared up frightened, flipping the ice cream to splatter against the windshield.

"You're a drunk, ignorant old Indian!" the little girl shrieked at him angrily.

"Bad White girl! Spoilin' nice blanket!" he mumbled, trying to wipe off the goo.

The girl leaned over him, opening the door on his side, and tried to push him out. "You don't know how to drive a car!"

"No drive," he admitted. But still he sat there stubborn and immovable.

Elsie frantically jumped out, ran around the car again, and managed to squeeze into the driver's seat. She turned the ignition key, rattled the gears. The car bucked forward, then backward. The old Indian lurched forward, bumping his head against the windshield.

"Crazy White girl! You no drive either!" He flung open the door. "I no goin'! I gettin' out!"

Before he could scramble out the other side, the car lurched violently forward, slapping the door shut. Elsie swung it out into the empty road. Peering to one side of the sticky blob on the windshield, she stepped on the gas.

Their flight had begun.

It was late afternoon when Freddie Dixon returned to the hotel suite. The early edition of the local paper, *The New Mexican*, had come out during his absence. Honey was seated on the living room couch, back toward him, avidly reading a copy. Dixon walked up behind her without greeting and bent down to read the black head on the front page:

MISSING CHILD REPORTED FLEEING

Underneath it was a one-column cut of Elsie. The lead paragraphs in bold type read:

The lost child reported to be missing since six o'clock last night is now believed to have run away with a considerable sum of money stolen from her mother.

She is Elsie Wilbur, ten-year-old daughter of Mrs. Honey Wilbur, a Fiesta visitor registered at La Fonda Hotel. She was last seen, according to police authorities, following an unidentified Indian from the Palace of the Governors. . .

Dixon had no opportunity to read further. Honey threw the paper on the floor and turned on him angrily.

"There wasn't any need for you to tell them that! It's a lie anyway. Elsie didn't steal that money. She took it in front of me and everybody because she knew she was welcome to it." She paused for breath, glaring at him. "Why shouldn't she have some money to have fun with during Fiesta? Didn't we go out, too? Isn't she my daughter? What's mine is hers. Richard said so!"

"Of course she took that money! You didn't give it to her, did you?" Dixon flopped down on the couch and stretched out his legs. "Honey, a kid with all that money isn't going to hang around the Plaza. She's going to go places and do things, and that roll of bills is the best trail she could leave. That's why I had to take the responsibility of mentioning it."

Honey walked to the window and looked out anxiously, then slowly strolled back. "Elsie's not your responsibility, Freddie. She's mine. And I won't have you trying to ruin her reputation. You act as if you hate her."

[39]

"How could I hate a small child? But she's got to be disciplined somehow, and pretty soon."

In the bright afternoon sun, the same photograph of Elsie stared from the top front page of a stack of papers mounted in a rack outside a weathered crossroads store and filling station. Grinning with pleasure, Elsie stood before it. At a gas pump behind her Inocencio was watching the attendant filling the car. Elsie turned around and beckoned to him.

When the old Indian came up, she pointed proudly at the cut and giggled. "That's me! It looks just like me, too! Doesn't it?"

Inocencio looked at the photo and then at the girl without answering. Like most Indians, he abhorred photographic images. Each one took away a little of the original; when one was photographed too much, he lost his face, like people in moving pictures.

"You don't know what it says about me, do you?" the girl taunted. "I'll bet you can't even read!"

"Nobody don't like you at home? So you runnin' away?" he asked quietly.

"Everybody hates me and I hate them!" the girl broke out spitefully. "They're not going to catch me!" She knelt down and scribbled quickly on the back of a picture postcard she had bought inside the store.

"Nobody like me, too, but I goin' home! That where I belong!" Inocencio drew his blanket closer about him, and started to walk out to the highway that stretched straight and endlessly across the desert from one blue horizon to another bluer and farther still.

Elsie jumped up, and running after him caught him by the arm. "Know what that says?" she demanded, thrusting the postcard under his nose. "It tells everybody I'm going away with you!" Jerking it back, she ran to drop it in a mail box outside the store.

Inocencio's slow mind was still grappling with the appalling significance of this when Elsie marched back derisively. "You're not going home now! Unless you want to be locked up in jail for stealing the car!"

The old man stared helplessly at the girl, then at the attendant walking up to them. "White girl pay," he said in a quiet, passive voice.

"White girl pay! I say!" Elsie mocked him with the familiar refrain, digging out money from the little satin purse swung on her arm. She walked toward the car, calling bossily over her shoulder, "Come on!"

Climbing into the driver's seat, she stacked a couple of pillows and an old lap robe beneath and behind her so she could more easily reach the pedals with her short legs. Inocencio clambered in beside her, staring fixedly at the fat little purse the girl had laid down on the seat between them. Without noticing his look, Elsie took up her purse and started the car. It rolled slowly out into the highway, heading westward across the wide, empty desert—the girl ridiculously small and the old Indian looming large and solid beside her . . .

The sun was sinking now and the redrock cliffs, faded as the old Indian's blanket, began to glow and deepen in color. They were no longer sparse, solitary islands floating in a sea of sage, but long reefs walling the highway from northern winds. At their far end a low cloud of grimy black smoke stained the clear sky.

"We gettin' there," said Inocencio.

The drive had been long and tiresome for Elsie, even though it had been easy enough to steer the car on the straight and free highway. Her back ached, her eyes were tired. Now she sat up nervously alert to confront the increasing traffic.

"We here," said Inocencio as they entered the town.

Gallup was an ugly town, as tough as one could find anywhere. A trading center for Zuni and Navajo Indians who rode in from

[41]

their immense reservations. A frontier town still enlivened by a scatter of cowpokes and sheepherders on Saturday nights. And with coal deposits in a nearby hogback to fuel locomotives, a small mining center for Slavs and Italians. Railroad Avenue expressed it all. On one side stretched the taut steel rails pounded intermittently night and day by great locomotives, sinewy lines of boxcars and lengths of gleaming silver Pullmans hurtling past with poignant and haunting shrieks against the empty and lonely immensities of timeless space; rushing by with the grimy smell of smoke and cinders always so redolent of the far off, romantic and unreal. On the other side, the road was flanked by a row of greasy little lunch-rooms, ghastly lit bars, pool rooms and tawdry stores; by fire-trap hotels, dollar flophouses, and four-bit throws. Across it sauntered railroad men to while away time between runs. Miners swinging empty lunch pails plodded tiredly in from work. On the corners stood Spanish-Americans with sad black eyes and bitter mouths, resentful of being called Mexicans. Everywhere wandered Indians. They slithered aimlessly along the walks in dusty moccasins with twinkling silver buttons; squatted along the walls nursing babies and picking out lice from their hair; reeled drunkenly into the gutters as if already trying to escape the inevitable club of White authority. And in all their faces, the Brown, the White, the Red, there was the same quality of alien remoteness that was the town itself. Gallup was an ugly town, isolated in illimitable space, de-fenseless against the scorching heat, freezing cold, and blasting wind of its high plateau. Yet all this misery, poverty, and shabby sinfulness was but a tawdry facade hiding from the heartless an invisible beauty that endured as if under a protective and phantas-mal spell cast by the strange dark wings hovering above it. All its quarreling races and breeds—the Wops and Dagoes, Greasers, Gringos, and Redskins—seemed bound together here as nowhere else by this mysterious beauty, this strange enchantment, that had drawn them here to attest the truth of their common humanness.

Inocencio had expressed it all in two words. "We here."

Elsie swung the stolen blue sedan into Railroad Avenue. It was sunset now, and in the evening rush hour the street was crowded. A traffic jam had been created; cars were backed up at the stop signal ahead. At the wail of a siren she straightened up to attention. A motorcycle cop was roaring toward them on the other side of the street in pursuit of a traffic violator.

"He won't catch me!" Elsie shrieked, stepping on the gas. She swerved out of her own lane of traffic, throwing Inocencio against the door. He righted himself, clutching at the dashboard, as Elsie wildly forced other cars aside, burst through the stop signal, and leapt free of traffic. A block past the railroad crossing a grove of trees stood between the highway and the railroad tracks. Elsie rammed the car into the thick brush and jumped out. Throwing the key away, she grabbed Inocencio by the blanket. "Come on!"

"Crazy White girl! That policeman not after you!" he grumbled, crawling out.

"This is a hot car! We've got to ditch it!" she shouted in a childish and melodramatic voice.

They ran through the brush, and guiltily looking behind them slowly crossed the railroad tracks. They came out on Third Street, which crossed the Santa Fe tracks and the dry, sandy creek bed and led north into the Navajo Reservation past a gaunt mercantile establishment in whose high facade stood an old-fashioned, Hiawatha-style, wooden Indian with paint-peeled feathers. This marked the historic Indian trading area.

Inocencio and Elsie walked slowly up the street past more great wholesale mercantile houses dealing in sheep pelts, wool and cattle hides; old adobe and wooden-front trading posts stacked to the ceiling with Navajo blankets, the stock commodity; dreary retail stores cluttered with cheap supplies for the Indian trade; and greasy cafes bootlegging rotgut whiskey. The sun was setting, and in its lurid red flare the dust churned up by passing wagons and

[43]

pickups was thick enough to cut with a knife. Through it swarmed Indians of every description: slim, dark Navajos in Levi's and wearing turquoise earrings; moon-faced women in brilliant velveteen blouses and billowing gingham skirts; a few Apaches in tall peaked hats; occasional broad-faced Zunis. Dirty, peaked children with red-rimmed eyes were staring hungrily through the greasy cafe windows. A woman, loaded down with silver jewelry, was squatting in the gutter suckling her child. Whole family groups stood forlornly on the corners.

Elsie drew closer to Inocencio as a drunken Apache reeled down the walk. The cheap, tawdry and stark realism of the street already frightened her as much as its barbaric color and alien strangeness fascinated her. It was the reverse side of playtime, tourist New Mexico; the commercial, workday warp underlying the decorative woof of all fiestas; the Skid Row of the 25,000 square-mile Navajo Reservation.

Inocencio was no stranger to it. He said simply, "I hungry!"

Elsie followed him without protest into a lunch counter squeezed between two store buildings. Under the harsh light of an unshaded electric light globe her little face looked white, pinched and drawn with fatigue. Her legs and puny arms ached from stretching for wheel and pedals. She was too tired to refuse the bowl of watery soup and the hamburger fried in rancid grease set before her. Yet unappetizing as they were, they calmed her nervous excitability and restored her strength. She slid off the stool, paid the bill without protest, and with polite reassurance laid a quarter on the dirty counter.

"What do yeh want now?" grumbled the unshaven proprietor, looking up over the bib of his greasy apron.

Inocencio grabbed the coin up and thrust it into the girl's hand as they went out the door. "You leavin' that money behind for nothin'!"

Elsie gave a short, derisive laugh. "Why, you don't even know what a tip is!"

They strolled aimlessly up the twilit street and stopped on the corner. "Where are we going, Inocencio?" Elsie asked finally.

"Sleepin' somewheres mebbe," the old Indian said vaguely after a time.

"But where?" Elsie asked sharply.

"That woman I know mebbe," he answered cryptically.

They crossed the street, and in the thickening twilight walked slowly toward Sand Flat, a slum area along the creek bed. The stores and loading platforms gave way to crumbling box adobes and wooden shacks where petty White thieves bought stolen goods; Mexicans shacked up with whores of three races; and decadent Navajos bought liquor, peyote and marijuana. Inocencio finally stopped before a stretch of sand littered with tin cans where stood four or five one-room huts and a wooden toilet clustered about a courtyard strung with lines of washing.

"I talk with that woman I knowin'. You give me money."

"I'll pay. White girl pay!" Elsie said niggardly.

Inocencio stubbornly kept his hand outstretched. "That woman don't know White girl. Mebbe she 'fraid. You stayin' here."

"How much?" the girl asked suspiciously.

"Two dollars. One dollar more she don't talk about nothing."

Inocencio took the three dollars she dug out of her purse, walked to one of the huts, and knocked. A slatternly, bony Mexican woman came out. They talked. Then Inocencio beckoned to Elsie.

When Elsie walked up, the woman gave her a sharp, distrustful look. "She's too young. Much trouble!"

"No trouble. It O.K." said Inocencio confidently.

"O.K.? No?" the woman demanded of the girl.

"It's O.K. He paid you, didn't he?" Elsie asked arrogantly.

The woman shrugged and led them to an empty hut. She pushed open the door, watched Inocencio and Elsie enter, then plodded back across the courtyard. Halfway across she looked up to see a Navajo standing in the doorway of an opposite hut. Slimly built, he wore a filthy shirt and Levi's, and his hair was tied with a rag into a chignon falling to one shoulder. His face was splotched and wore the cunning and evil look of depravity. The woman hesitated. "*Cuidado!* Mind your own business!" she yelled at him and went on back to her hut. The Navajo remained in the doorway staring at the hut into which Elsie and Inocencio had entered.

Inside, the old man and the girl looked about them. In one corner was a decrepit bed covered with a few grimy blankets. In the other stood a small and greasy wood-stove. There was one small, bare window. Underneath it was set a rude plank table on which were stacked a few cracked dishes and a paper shoe box containing tin forks and knives. On the bare plank floor was a single straw mat—a fraying *petate.*

"It isn't very nice," Elsie complained. "It's dirty. The maid hasn't even changed the bed!"

Inocencio stolidly squatted down on the *petate*, legs crossed underneath him, Indian fashion, and drew his blanket around him with a gesture of aloofness. "No good," he assented, staring out the open door into the darkening courtyard. "No nice big trees. No nice fresh water runnin' by."

Elsie plumped down on the squeaky bed, her purse falling out of her pocket. Inocencio, noticing it, licked his dry lips. "Drivin' all day make me sick. Mebbe have little drink. Feel good."

Elsie casually noticed her purse and picked it up. Suddenly she bounced up and down on the squeaky bed, flopped on her back, and kicked her feet up in the air.

"Anyway we're here!" she cried with childish delight. "We've

[46]

run away and stolen a car and we haven't been caught! That'll show 'em!"

Inocencio remained staring glumly out the open door. The Navajo was still standing, faintly visible in the dusk, in the doorway of his own hut across the courtyard.

About ten o'clock the next morning Sheriff Mann and Shorty Thompson were waiting in their office with a Spanish workman in overalls when Honey and Dixon rushed in.

"You've located my daughter!" Honey cried excitedly. "Where is she? And the man who's come to claim the reward! He . . . "

The sheriff gently pushed the workman forward. "This is Mr. Baca, Mrs. Wilbur. And Mr. Dixon. We haven't found your child yet. But Mr. Baca here saw her Wednesday night in a roadside lunchroom near the turn off to Tewa Pueblo."

"Was she all right? Did she . . . "

"Sí, Señora," said the workman hastily. "But the money, Señora? It makes an hour that I have waited. I must get back to my job, Señora."

"Now wait a minute!" Dixon interrupted. "That reward was posted for information leading to the girl's return. Not for any· body who just saw her two days ago!"

Mr. Baca drew himself up stiffly. "Señor! The niña refused my offer to return to her casa in my pickup. You, Señor, now refuse the money the radio said you would give me. No! I will not talk!"

Shorty had finished rolling a cigarette and now stuck it into his mouth. "Wal, I reckon ever'body else is doin' it for you."

[47]

The sheriff spread his hands for quiet, and turned to Honey. "Now Mrs. Wilbur. Perhaps Mr. Baca is not entitled to receive your reward—yet. He only saw your child. Still his information is most valuable. It may be worth a token payment if you . . . "

Honey, with an impatient and careless gesture, thrust a ten-dollar bill into the workman's hands. Immediately his face broke into a smile. Honey led him off to the far end of the room where the other men could not hear her excited questioning.

Sheriff Mann sat down at his desk and resumed talking to Shorty and Dixon. "The city police reported that the girl was seen leaving the Plaza behind an unidentified Indian on Wednesday evening. This man Baca confirms it. The girl was in Maria's lunchroom with an Indian an hour or so later and rode away in a wagon with him." He leaned toward Shorty. "Now, Shorty, that Maria ought to be able to identify the Indian." He motioned toward Baca. "He tells me they knew each other. Then go to the pueblo. Somebody must have seen them during the dance next day if they were still there. Check with the state police who was on duty there, too."

The three men rose as Honey and Baca walked up. "She's not lost. She has run away—just like you said, Freddie."

"We'll find her, Mrs. Wilbur, thanks to Mr. Baca here," the sheriff said.

The workman politely shook hands all around and left. Shorty pushed his battered Stetson to the back of his head. "I figure there must be a durn good reason fer a tike to run off from her mammy. Now what do you reckon it is?"

"Because she's always doing it!" snapped Dixon.

Dixon took Honey by the arm, with a nod at the sheriff, and led her out to the sidewalk.

"She willfully ran away from me! She even refused to let that nice man bring her home—at night, too!" Honey sniffled as Dixon looked up and down the street for a taxi. "Oh, you were right,

Freddie! I didn't mean all those hateful things I said to you. I'm sorry, Freddie."

"They'll catch her. Don't worry . . . What we need now is a stiff drink and some breakfast. Then I'll make sure Evans follows up on the search."

"But she's been gone two nights now. Where? Where could she be all this time? And why, Freddie?"

Dixon threw up his arm. A taxi rolled up. They got in and rode away.

Late that afternoon Elsie and Inocencio walked out of El Morro, the little movie house on Gallup's main business street, Coal Avenue. The morning had been too long and boring in their squalid hut on Sand Flat, and Elsie had insisted on going into town to her afternoon movie. As she came out, blinking at the light, her clothes showed that they had been slept in for two nights. The tidy white batiste dress was grimy and wrinkled. Her patent leather slippers were cracked and scuffed, her pink bobby socks black with dirt. Even her hair was uncombed, one pigtail tied with a piece of string. But her happy face showed that she had been delighted with the picture. She stopped to buy a bag of popcorn. Then she and Inocencio strolled slowly down the street looking in shop windows.

"That was a good movie, wasn't it, Inocencio?"

The old Indian was bored and glum. "These movin' pitchers! White people kissin' and makin' love all a time!"

The little girl giggled and offered him the bag of popcorn.

Inocencio sullenly waved the sack aside. "You eatin' all day! I no like candy and peanuts. I tired of them cold sandwiches White people eat. Good meat cookin' on fire. That what Indian like. I hungry!"

[49]

Farther down the block he complained again. "Ice cream. Cold soda pop. Agh! I needin' little drink to warm my belly. That good!"

A siren began to wail; a motorcycle cop was racing down the street toward them. Elsie grabbed Inocencio and dragged him into the entrance of a clothing store. Huddling against the window with alarm, they watched the cop whiz by. Elsie grinned and stuffed some more popcorn in her mouth.

"We goin' now," said Inocencio.

But Elsie's fancy was caught by some children's outfits displayed in the window. "Ooh look, Inocencio! Let's go in!" She tugged at his blanket.

"I waitin' here," the old Indian stubbornly insisted.

In a little while the girl came out beaming with an armful of packages. "Wait'll you see what I bought! Just wait, Inocencio!"

The old man did not answer. They plodded back down the hill to Railroad Avenue and across the tracks to the tawdry Indian trading area. Inocencio stopped in front of a market. "I hungry! We buyin' meat. I cook him myself!"

"Let's get a sandwich and a coke then."

"No! I hungry! You givin' me some money. I say it!"

There was a stubborn command in his voice that Elsie could not ignore. She opened her purse and started to thumb through the bills inside like a penurious little housewife. Suddenly she thrust it back into her pocket. "I'll go in, too! They might charge you too much!"

Inocencio stalked sullenly into the store, Elsie following at his heels. A slab of meat, bread, coffee, jam . . . The little girl protested each purchase, stingily doling out money from her purse.

"You eatin' all day! I eatin' now!" The old man was insistent.

They walked slowly home across Sand Flat to their hut, each carrying an armful of packages. Elsie gleefully threw her bundles on the unkempt bed and began to rip open the paper. "Turn your back now, Inocencio! Promise you won't look!"

"I not lookin'!" The old Indian surlily unwrapped the food at the table, then scrounged around to find a greasy frying pan and a blackened coffee pot.

Elsie behind him slipped her begrimed dress over her head, exposing her thin little body in its childish pink panties and embroidered undershirt. A sweet, innocent looking little child now, she grabbed for her new clothes.

Inocencio, back turned toward her, poked down the ashes in the stove with a noisy rattle and bang. "I get wood now!" Holding the edge of his blanket up over his face so he would not see Elsie, he stalked out the door and across the courtyard.

The Navajo drew back inside his doorway as Inocencio passed, then again peered out toward the hut where the old Pueblo Indian and girl were quartered. In a few minutes he was rewarded by a surprising and charming sight. It was Elsie standing in the doorway, dressed up in a child's cowboy suit: a gaudy shirt and little blue Levi trousers with red facings, a decorative pair of small boots, and a wide-brimmed hat with a fancy band. Peeking around to make sure that Inocencio was out of sight, she ran quickly across the courtyard past the Navajo's hut, and stuffed something in a big trash can standing beside the outside toilet. Then she skipped quickly back.

When she was out of sight, the Navajo strolled out of his hut as if he were going to the toilet. With a quick look around to make sure he was not observed, he grabbed the bundle out of the trash can and hurried back to his hut. Inside his doorway, he unfolded it. It was Elsie's discarded dress. With a look of perverted passion on his besotted face, he pressed it against him, stroking out its wrinkles. Abruptly he drew back out of sight.

Inocencio was coming back across the courtyard with an armful of kindling and a filled water bucket. Entering his own hut he was confronted by Elsie posturing in her new cowboy suit. "How do you like it?" she shouted in a proud, childish voice. "I'm a cowboy now!"

"Ai, ai, ai," he muttered kindly but gruffly, and went about his business of building a fire in the stove and putting on the steak and coffee.

Elsie buckled around her thin waist a little imitation leather belt with colored glass studs and a toy pistol in a tiny holster. While supper was cooking, she strutted around the room admiring herself and snapping the lead pistol at the furniture. She stopped suddenly. "Inocencio! Where's my animals? I want to shoot my animals!"

The old Indian turned around from the smoking stove with an angry look. "White people get gun. Shoot animals for fun. When has it been different?" His accusing eyes softened as he stared at her childish figure. "You leavin' them animals in that car when we run away, I think." He turned back to his work, setting out on the table the cracked plates and tin forks and knives.

It was sunset when they ate. Inocencio was ravenous. Elsie picked lightly at her supper, already selfishly full of candy bars, popcorn, Popsicles and sodas, and her mind on her new cowboy suit. Finally, the old Indian emptied his plate and slid it back with a grunt. But he was not quite satisfied; he had not had a drink for two days. "Good! Mebbe have little drink now. That better!"

Elsie ignored the hint. She got up and walked to the doorway. The sun was setting across the dreary sand flat. All the huts had been rented, and some Mexicans and their girls were crowding one of the doorways. A drinking party was beginning. She could hear their loud voices and the noisy tinkle of glasses and bottles.

Inocencio remained sitting at the table. An eager look of triumph flitted across his dark, somber face. There was Elsie's little satin purse, dropped on the floor beside her scuffed slippers when she was changing clothes. This was the opportunity Inocencio had been waiting for. He stealthily reached down and deftly slipped out some money. He rose and walked to the doorway.

"I comin' right back," he muttered, walking out past her as if going to the toilet. Reaching it, he threw a quick glance back over his shoulder, then slid swiftly around the side and vanished into the gathering dusk.

When Inocencio returned, Elsie was sitting disconsolate and lonely on the stoop. Across the darkening courtyard came a roar of drunken laughter from the drinking party. The big Indian walked past her without greeting and lit the kerosene lamp on top of the stove. In its dim flicker his slightly flushed, dark face showed that he had grabbed a quick drink or two. He squatted down on the *petate*, legs crossed under him, and boldly took another drink from the pint of cheap whiskey he had brought back with him.

Elsie followed him in and plopped down on the decrepit bed without speaking. Both escapees now faced the drab realities of their foolish flight. The excitement of running away in a stolen car had worn off. The little girl was disgusted with her squalid surroundings and secretly wished she were back in her mother's comfortable hotel suite. Inocencio too was bored at being cooped up, pining to be back under his big cottonwoods beside the running stream. They stared at each other covertly with all the inherent antagonism created by their differences in age, sex, race and temperaments.

Elsie, noticing her purse, picked it up and shrewdly thumbed through the bills it contained. "You stole two dollars, Inocencio!"

[53]

she shouted accusingly at the old Indian on the floor in front of her. "You're a thief! You're an old drunk Indian, besides!"

He sheepishly dug beneath his blanket and drew out some coins to hand her. "Here the change. I forget him." Hearing another burst of drunken laughter outside, he nodded toward the courtyard. "They havin' a drink. Me too!" He tipped up the bottle he had bought for another swig.

"I don't like people when they're tight!" complained Elsie. "That's why I don't like Freddie. He's always tight and making my mother tight. They're probably tight right now. Having another cocktail party—like those people across the way."

The sound of a high-pitched whorish scream followed by more ribald laughter was hardly a fair comparison with the polite restraint of Honey's cocktail parties, but it betrayed to Inocencio what Elsie thought of them and where her thoughts were.

"We goin' home?" he asked hopefully.

"And be put in jail? Are you crazy? No! They won't ever find us!"

She jumped up and stalked restlessly around the room in her new little boots. Every so often she stopped, crouched, and jerked out her toy pistol to fire at Inocencio in childish imitation of Western movie cowboys. The old Indian calmly ignored her, taking out the pint from his blanket for another swig. Elsie stopped to berate him again.

"You won't play with me! Even Mary does sometimes. But you won't because you're old and drunk and lazy. You're not any fun!"

The drinks inside him finally goaded Inocencio into answering her fishwife nagging. "White people always playin' like movin' pitchers. Always talkin'. Indian don't talk much, but he mean what he say."

Elsie looked at him contemptuously. "Indians aren't anybody! I thought they wore pretty feathers in their hair. You don't even wear a hat! You've got pigtails like a girl!"

She backed away, whipped out her toy pistol again, and shot him. "Bang! Fall dead! I'm playing Cowboy and Indian, and the Cowboys always kill all the Indians!"

Rapid-fire, she pulled the trigger a dozen times. Her eyes were hard, her face distorted. This was more than childish play-acting. All the antagonism between them was coming out. She had the will to kill with a real gun.

The old Indian sat humped in his blanket, a shrouded pyramid. In his simple nature there was much of the child—and the animal, too. He felt the girl's bitterness, hate, and wish to kill; and they roused in him the old, atavistic hate of the Indian for the White who had destroyed his people. Deliberately, he set down his pint bottle on the floor and unfolded his blanket.

The simple gesture stopped the little girl. In all the time they had been together, she had never seen him with his blanket off. Now in his dirty shirt and ragged trousers upheld by a wide leather belt in whose silver buckle glowed a single chunk of turquoise, he looked different. He was no longer soft, womanly, and somehow anonymous in a blanket. The outline of his figure stood out; his broad-shouldered body was strong and hard. As the girl stood watching him, he withdrew a long, naked knife from his belt with his dark, brown hand, and tested its edge with his thumb.

"Ai," he said in his soft, low voice. "White men got guns. Shoot Indians way off like animals. For fun. They no get close to Indian's knife. It sharp!" He flipped it suddenly to the floor between them where it embedded itself tremblingly in the plank, shimmering in the lamplight.

The little girl shuddered in her cowboy suit. She too felt the difference between the naked steel of personal combat and the long-range, romantic and impersonal warfare of the movies. Morbidly fascinated, she watched him pick up her slipper and begin to whet the knife slowly and rhythmically on its thin sole.

"What do you think you're going to do with that knife?" she

demanded with a little of her old arrogance. But she holstered her toy pistol and sat down stiffly on the bed.

Inocencio was through talking. He took another gulp from the bottle, then resumed whetting the long blade.

Fear crept over the girl now. "Inocencio! Stop it! Let's don't play any more! I'll tell my mother on you!"

It was night now; outside in the courtyard the whores and the Mexicans were getting noisier. She could hear the snatch of a song —"*La borrachita, me voy!*"—and the crash of breaking glass.

"I don't care what you do! I'm going to bed!" The girl tugged off her cowboy boots and dropped them on the floor, her eyes still furtively watching Inocencio. She hung her wide-brimmed hat on the foot-post of the bed. Then she draped her pistol belt over the head-post as if to have it within easy reach. There was something ludicrously funny and tragically pathetic in her childish, stereotyped actions. She crawled between the grimy blankets to lie still staring apprehensively at the old Indian.

A long time passed. Inocencio's dark mood passed, too. He put up his knife, set aside the bottle so he would have an eye-opener in the morning, and gathered the blanket around him again. Once again a shrouded pyramid, he sat in heavy silence. Not drunk after his heavy dinner, just comfortably tight.

In a little while he got up and blew out the lamp. Elsie could see him, dimly visible in the moonlight coming through the window, as he knelt clumsily down on the *petate* and folded his hands with full humility—a big, simple man with the heart of a child.

Elsie felt shamed. She could not forbear hurling at him a last taunt. "What do you think you're doing? I thought you were a heathen!"

Inocencio did not stir.

"I guess I can say my prayers just as well as an old Indian!" She hastily crawled out of bed and knelt down on the floor with clasped hands.

For a moment they knelt together. Inocencio finished first. He lay down on the *petate*, wrapping his blanket close around him. Elsie jumped back into bed. Two children, two outcasts, they drifted off to sleep.

Sometime after midnight the Navajo appeared at the window, cautiously standing sideways and peering into the room. The stream of moonlight angling through the window to the bed illumined his debauched face. The dark splotches stood out darker. The cheek and mouth muscles were twitching. The pupils of his eyes were dilated.

The room was still; the door was open. He could not see Inocencio sleeping on the floor directly below the window, but he could detect Elsie's body stretched out on the bed. The drinking party across the courtyard had devolved into an angry row. Elsie, awakened by the racket, roused on one elbow and listened sleepily. Then she flopped back down and rolled over, face to the wall.

The Navajo lewdly ran his tongue over his dry, twitching lips and stepped back. A moment later he reappeared, peeking in the door. Softly he stepped inside. Then, blinded with pent-up passion, he hurled himself full length upon the girl in bed.

She let out the frightened cry of a child in a nightmare. "Mother!" And then another. "Mary!" Wrestling in the thin moonlight, fully awakened now, she glimpsed the face of her assailant. "Inocencio!"

The old Indian was awakened instantly by her terrified shriek of appeal. He jumped to his feet, his mind still a little befuddled. The Navajo, clawing back the covers from the writhing girl, gave a grunt of surprise and rage. He leapt off the bed, hurling himself at Inocencio just as the old man threw off his blanket. Both men went down, trying to fight free of its entangling folds.

Elsie watched them, paralyzed with fear. She could not see them clearly as they rolled against the stove, knocking off the dishes and the frying pan with a noisy crash. But they were not fighting as she once had seen two White men fight—getting to their feet and striking out with both fists. Each was striving desperately to get at the other's throat or to free an arm to get at his knife.

They rolled back into the shaft of moonlight. It was clear to her that the young, lithe, and hopped-up Navajo was quicker than the older, slightly befuddled Pueblo Indian. But Inocencio was stronger, and his weight was gradually forcing the intruder down. The Navajo suddenly twisted free, squirming to his knees above Inocencio. His hand whipped to his belt. In the moonlight she could see the bright flicker of his raised knife. Its striking arc was stopped abruptly in mid-air as Inocencio's right leg shot up and out in a powerful kick to the groin. The knife whirled through the air; Elsie could hear it clatter metallically against the stove across the small room.

The Navajo flopped jarringly on his back with a grunt of pain. In that instant Inocencio's own hand was freed to jerk out his knife. She could see it whip up above his head. Then lurching forward, he plunged it into the Navajo's breast.

There was an instant of gaping silence made more terrible by a faint, dying gasp from the Navajo and the hoarse, wheezy panting of Inocencio standing above him. It was broken by Elsie's terrified scream of comprehension. There followed it, like an echo, another scream from across the courtyard and an angry shout. "*Siléncio! Madre de Dios! No podemos dormir!*"

Inocencio struck a match, lit the lamp. His face in the glow was dark and somber. With a strange dignity sharpened by an immediate and ruthless acceptance of reality, he stooped, pulled out his knife, and wiped the blade clean on the Navajo's trousers. Sheathing it, he picked up his blanket to throw around his shoulders. Only then did he turn to face Elsie.

[58]

The little girl was standing on the bed, huddled against the wall in a posture of abject terror. It was significant that she was not looking at the Navajo's body. She was staring at Inocencio with wild eyes beseeching some mercy and compassion, perhaps even some help and comfort. Something in the old Indian's grave, inscrutable face lent her the assurance to step tremblingly down from the bed. Inocencio in one motion jerked off a blanket and flung it over the body on the floor.

The little cowboy and the big, blanketed Indian now stood facing each other as if alone. Yet the presence of death stood with them, invisible but deeply felt. It was the moment of truth between their secret and essential selves, stripped now of all differences in age, sex, race and temperament. They looked at each other as if seeing for the first time their common humanness. What happens at such a moment? No one knows. Only the heart speaks, in wordless silence.

The little girl moved, haltingly, a slow step forward. The big Indian, arms hanging at side, grasped the edges of his blanket and held it open. It was the immemorial tribal gesture of one who opens to another his heart, his home, and accepts the responsibility of giving his life if need be to protect them.

Elsie flung herself against him. Inocencio sank slowly to his knees, his long arms wrapping her in the folds of his blanket. The little girl ceased to tremble. Her thin arms crept round his neck. She suddenly laid her head upon his shoulder. It was the victory of a little, lost, and fatherless girl who in this tent-like blanket had found at last a spiritual home and someone she could utterly trust. It was the surrender, too, of a woman who acknowledged the will and strength of a man's protection. In the dim, flickering glow of the lamp neither moved nor spoke.

Day broke with an explosive sunburst whose bright flare lit up a cloudless sky and a vast, treeless expanse of upland desert. As far as the eye could see, the sage-gray plateau spread out, imperceptibly sloping upward toward a high, blue range on the horizon. Across it, straight as a string, stretched a single narrow road. Along this moved a solitary spot of bright color in the immense landscape. It was a pickup in whose bed squatted a family of Navajos: a slim, arrogant man wearing a red headband; a fat, moon-faced woman in a green velveteen shirt and a flounced orange skirt; and several children.

After a time another spot appeared on the road ahead. The pickup slowed down and stopped beside two people waiting for a ride. One was a small White girl dressed in a child's cowboy suit. The other was a big, blanketed Pueblo Indian carrying a roll of grimy store blankets. They clambered quickly into the bed of the pickup with the others. The driver rattled his gears. The car drove on.

It was a fresh start, the beginning of another day.

Just after breakfast that morning a State Highway Patrol officer noticed a car rammed into the thick brush beside the road. He pulled in to look it over. Evidently the car had been abandoned in a hurry. The door was open and the ignition key was gone. There was nothing in it but a brown paper sack out of which had been spilled on the front seat a little clay deer, a skunk, squirrel, beaver and some other toy animals. Putting them back into the sack, he jotted down in his notebook the license plate number, title number and other details on the registration slip in a case wrapped round the steering post. Then he went back to his own car, parked alongside, and called in the information over his car radio.

"Dark blue sedan. White sidewalls. Unlocked. I can't find any keys . . . No. Nothing but a paper sack full of some Indian-made clay animals . . ."

Finishing his report, the officer waited a moment. Then a voice over the car radio ordered him to another assignment. "Right! Got it . . . Better drive over to Sand Flat now. A Navajo has just been reported murdered. Keep the crowd back. Pick up any details you can . . . Right! O.K. now!"

The officer switched off the radio, started up the car. It backed, then swung out upon the highway with its siren wailing. A crowd of nondescript Whites, Mexicans and Indians was already beginning to form when the officer drove up to the trash-littered court. All were staring with morbid fascination toward the hut in which lay the body of the slain Navajo.

The officer, shutting off siren and motor, got out and walked to the hut. He peeked quickly inside, closed the door, and authoritatively motioned the people back.

"Come on! Get back!"

There was a sudden shout. The scrawny and slatternly Mexican proprietress came running out of the hut in which the murdered Navajo had been living. She was carrying a bundle of rumpled white cloth. "*Madre de Dios!*" she wailed with righteous indignation.

The officer grabbed her by the arm as she ran up. "Here! Get back! Let's don't get excited . . . What's the trouble with you?"

The woman threw off his hand and dramatically shook out before him Elsie's discarded dress. "The *niña's* dress! In that dead man's house it was. Why? *Quién sabe?* Can she be naked, without clothes? How am I, a simple poor woman confronted with trouble, to know such strange things?"

"Now hold on . . . "

"Trouble! *Ay de mi!* I knew there would be trouble. They not only stick him with a knife. They run off with my blankets. Two! Not one, but two! Good blankets. Worth four dollars. Each one. And I am a poor woman who . . . "

The officer quietly reached out and took the dress from her.

"O.K. . . . O.K. They took your blankets." He folded up the dress and stuck it under his own arm. "Now what about this *niña?*"

The sun had climbed to high noon now, and was glaring down with blinding brilliance upon a remote trading post when another pickup rolled up and stopped beside a few others, some old Studebaker wagons, and a row of shaggy ponies tied to a hitching rack in front. The post was long and low, massively built of rock and adobe, with walls two feet thick and windows striped with iron bars. It sat back from the road, isolate and alone in the sea of sage beating against the far blue range.

Inocencio and Elsie climbed out of the pickup with the Navajos, and Inocencio said gravely to the driver, "I thankin' you. Now I buy my friends somethin' good. Mebbe soda pop."

The driver assented with a nod, leading his family toward the post. Inocencio and Elsie followed. Lounging in front of the doorway were more Navajos and a small group of Apaches wearing high-crowned hats. They drew back, refraining with traditional politeness from staring at the newcomers. Elsie shyly handed Inocencio her purse and followed him inside.

The huge room was dim and cool, cluttered with merchandise, and crowded with Navajos. It had a floor of hard, pressed adobe. The roof beams or vigas were great spruce logs hauled down from the mountains, darkened by the smoke of many years. Down one side and across the back stretched the long counter. Behind it lounged a nondescript White man—the trader—waiting trade and leisurely talking to the people who straggled in and out.

"Somethin' good" for Navajos was always a can of tomatoes. The trader opened one each for the two men and woman, and Inocencio handed a bottle of soda pop to each of the children. Finally, he took a bottle out of the big red container and handed it to Elsie with the dignified, authoritative manner of a host bestowing a gift to a child. Elsie took it shyly and gratefully as any other

[62]

child. There was a big-bellied stove in the center of the room surrounded by boxes of sand to spit in. They all stood around it in silence, greedily sucking pop and tomatoes. After a time the Navajo family gravely nodded to the big Pueblo Indian and the little White *Belicana*, and went back out to the pickup.

Inocencio was in no hurry at all. He bought himself and the girl a box of crackers and a thick slice of sausage. Then with Elsie at his heels, he strolled down the counter inspecting and pricing everything.

"Matches to light fire . . . Good coffee. Big can . . . I takin' them sheep ribs . . . You got some Navajo bread? . . . Chocolate cookies. Ai."

The trader laid each article down on the counter. Inocencio stuffed it in his blanket roll. "Sugar. Salt . . . Big picnic. Cowboy get hungry," he told the trader with a straight face. "Mebbe buyin' that cheese too."

The trader looked at Elsie and laughed. He took down a cellophane strip of lollipops and threw it on the pile. "Do you like these, cowboy? You can have them—free!"

"Yes!" said Elsie. "They're the kind I like! 'Pink Puppies'!"

Inocencio carefully counted out money to pay the bill and stuffed the little satin purse back into his pocket. Strolling on down the counter, he stopped suddenly in front of a worn .22-caliber rifle to which a faded paper tag was tied. He took it down, opened the breech with a practiced hand, and squinted down the barrel.

"Cowboy got gun. I got nothing to shoot." He put the rifle back.

The trader looked at the little toy pistol dangling in Elsie's holster and laughed again. Reading the faded tag on the rifle, he said, "This is an old rifle I took for pawn years ago, and the time's run out."

"Old gun," agreed Inocencio. "Can't shoot nothin' straight. Mebbe you sell him."

[63]

"I don't sell firearms in a trading post, you know. But it's only a twenty-two and probably you and the little cowboy could have a little fun shooting tin cans with it. I suppose you're with that party of archaeologists digging up by those old ruins?"

Inocencio did not answer. He took down the rifle again. "How much you sell him?"

The trader shrugged. "I suppose there's no harm in letting it go."

"Got no shells."

"There's a box around here somewhere, I guess."

"How much you sell him?" Inocencio repeated, more sharply.

Elsie, bored by their dickering, turned away to wander about the post, still sucking her bottle of soda pop. The big room was like none she had ever seen. A mere country store, it was still imbued with the appalling significance of its role when it had been the only trading post serving an area of perhaps a thousand square miles, an outpost of an alien culture in an unmarked wilderness, the sole agency through which were exchanged the values of two ways of life, and the first economic institution in Navajo country.

In the back Elsie could see the great canvas sacks filled with wool, the stacks of sheep pelts and goat hides brought in from the roaming flocks—a nomadic people's primary means of existence. She peeked in the rug room, stacked from floor to ceiling with the blankets they had woven from the wool. Hanging on the wall and spread out on the floor were the rare old *bayetas*, the brilliant Germantown weaves, the fine, striped Chief blankets. There were the coarse dogies sold to Apaches and cowpokes as serapes, the small saddle blankets, the beautiful Crystal and Two Gray Hills, a curious *Yei* blanket. Soft glowing red, deep indigo blue, simple white, black and gray; in simple stripes or in intricate patterns; with simple, bold designs whose origin could be identified at first glance; tight enough to hold water, to outwear a century; a native utilitarian commodity that had become a household necessity

[64]

throughout the West; and a work of art as distinctive of its time and place as a Gobelin tapestry or a Persian rug.

Wandering back, Elsie stared curiously at all the supplies the Navajos obtained in trade for these materials. The walls were flanked with shelves of staples and canned goods. The floor was littered with bushel baskets of onions and pinto beans, bags of flour, salt and sugar. From wooden posts hung bridles and cinches, a roping saddle. Overhead hung slabs of mutton ribs, strings of jerky, a *ristra* of dried chiles. Elsie stopped at a counter to stare with a group of Navajo women at bolts of rich, solid-color velveteen and lengths of flowered ginghams. She knelt down with some children in front of a candy case, staring at licorice sticks, jelly beans, gum drops and bubble gum. And now she was held entranced by the pawn jewelry for which the post acted as a bank depository: the glowing silver, the mellow turquoise, rings, bracelets, eardrops, huge squash blossom necklaces and heavy concho belts.

Yet it was the people who fascinated her most. The slim-hipped Navajo men with their dark, arrogant faces. The scrawny and the fat Navajo women in their numerous, flounced skirts and richly colored velveteen blouses, slithering around in their fawn-pink moccasins twinkling with silver buttons. And the tall, sober Apaches in their high, peaked hats. They were dirty, but there was about them a clean proudness of bearing Elsie had not noticed in those back on Sand Flat. She caught a whiff of their peculiar, spicy Indian smell, too. About them they all carried a barbaric strangeness, a curious aloofness, that frightened her a little. Even their sibilant whispers intensified their habitual silence.

Inocencio was still haggling with the trader. She wandered outside to loaf in the sunshine. More men were rolling cigarettes; women were gossiping; children were playing silently in the dirt. There was a sudden shout. Two boys were racing their ponies across the sandy plain. Elsie could see their loose black hair streaming in the wind. One of the horses was a buckskin. The other was a pinto. The boy was riding it bareback, and Elsie could see the big splotch of black on its side. It was the shape of South America in one of her picture books at home. How fast they came, heels dug in, quirts flashing! They swept by in a cloud of dust.

"South America won! He beat!" she yelled, jumping up and down, clapping her hands.

None of the Navajos spoke. None of them looked at her. Elsie stuck her hands in her cowboy pants and was still. In a little while she sat down and watched the Indians, and stared at the blue mountains rising beyond the post. It was all relaxed and pleasant, the equivalent of a New England village green. But it was strange and mysterious, too. What made it so Elsie did not know. She only knew that she had left the White world far behind, and that this was a strange Indian world she had never seen and would always remember.

Soon Inocencio came out carrying his rifle and other purchases wrapped up in his fat roll of blankets. With him was a tall Apache in a new, high black hat. Elsie got up and walked toward them.

"We goin' now," Inocencio said simply.

The girl followed them to the Apache's old wagon. Inocencio and the Apache got onto the plank seat. Elsie scrambled into the box behind them. The Apache whipped up his team of broomtails. Drawing away from the post, they headed across the sage toward the rising blue mountains.

Honey and Dixon were having lunch with the two Evanses in the cantina of La Fonda. It was not yet noon and the hotel was jammed with a weekend crowd pouring into Santa Fe to climax

Fiesta. People stood three deep at the bar, and more kept crowding into the patio and lobby, waiting for the Indian entertainers to begin dancing. The day was Saturday, the third day since Elsie had disappeared, and the strain was telling on Honey. She picked at her lunch without appetite and kept ordering more cocktails.

"This damned Fiesta! Will it never end! I'm sick of seeing these fat rumps wobble by in imitation-leather *charro* pants!" she complained in a voice already thick. "This whole year's been nothing but one Goddamned, everlasting fiesta. I'd like to run away from it like Elsie. A flight from fiesta. That's what she's done. Run away from all this dressed-up, make-believe, boring fun!"

"Keep hold of yourself, Honey," said Dixon. "If you can just get into the spirit of it, it'll help to keep your mind off her."

"Look, the Indians are coming in now," said Margaret. "You'll love their dancing."

Honey twisted around to see a dignified old Indian, wrapped in a blanket, beginning to pound a drum. Four dancers stepped forth, knees lifting high, to wheel in front of him. All were painted a golden copper, and wore short embroidered kirtles and full-beaded moccasins. Straps of bells jingled on their muscular legs. In their right hands they shook gourd rattles. Two of them wore high headdresses of eagle feathers tipped with red yarn. The other two wore porcupine and deer hair roaches on their heads. Only as each completed the revolving circle could one see the great circular sun-wheels of brilliantly colored feathers pinned to their backs, catching the light and seeming themselves to revolve like flaming wheels. Suddenly one of the dancers lifted his rattle high, threw back his head, and gave a piercing cry. "Hi-yah!" The drum beat faster. The wheel turned more swiftly.

Honey pitched her voice above the pounding of feet and drum. "Why she'd run off with an Indian I don't know! An English chauffeur, an Algerian chef, yes! But one of these painted savages…"

[67]

"But they're not savages, Honey. Just costumed entertainers," protested Margaret soothingly.

The dance was authentically Indian enough, originally a Pawnee war dance derived from the old scalp dances on the Great Plains and now adopted by the southwestern Pueblos purely for tourist entertainment. So too had the costumes been adopted. Feather headdresses were never common to the Pueblos. With their beaded headbands supporting eagle feathers and downy eagle plumes, they had been Plains indications of sacredness or high rank, later used by women for "Indian Princess" contests. The back bustle, or great feathered sunwheel, was the traditional "crow belt" designating Plains warriors, like the insignia of the porcupine and deer hair roach. The Pueblos themselves, acknowledging their borrowing while still maintaining their own conventional and rigidly stylized dance-forms, humorously called themselves at these times "fancy dancers". And yet as the dancers pounded the floor with intricate footwork, great proud birds wheeling before her, Honey sensed in them a barbaric strangeness and savage frenzy that roused in her all the unconscious fears of childhood.

"I want another drink!" she shouted.

She was tight, noisy, and making a nuisance of herself. Even the Indians, stopping for a break, threw her dark looks of annoyance as they gathered around the old drummer.

Evans gave Dixon a warning nudge. "Do you think you should let her have another, wrought up as she is?"

The question was answered by another disturbance. The old drummer had taken up his drumstick again. The dancers, wiping off their sweaty faces, took up some buckskin shields, lifted their rattle arms. But only to be interrupted by Honey's maid, Mary, who came pushing through the crowd. Catching a glimpse of Honey, she broke through the dancers, bumping into one of them. He swung around with an angry face, but Mary was rushing across the floor to thrust a picture postcard into Honey's hands.

"The mail's just come and brought this! Oh, Mrs. Wilbur!"

Honey looked hazily at the picture on its face, then turned it over to read the childish scrawl on back: "Captured by Indians. Elsie."

The Indian dance was beginning another phase. The four dancers split into two pairs of fighting warriors. On their left arms they now wore round, white buckskin shields on which were painted stylized symbols. For weapons they still carried in their right hands the ominously rattling gourds. Great prancing gamecocks, they crouched low, lifting their shields. Each advanced warily upon his opponent in a quick dance step. The shields touched, the gourd rattles feinted and struck. Then whirling away, the sunwheels on their backs spread like angry tail feathers, the warriors came at each other again. One pair danced out into the lobby. The other, with quick ironic glances at each other, danced toward the woman who had been distracting them and their audience.

Honey, lips trembling, was staring transfixed at Elsie's postcard. "Captured by Indians! Oh my God!"

There sounded beside her a sudden ear-splitting war whoop. She flung back to look up into a grotesquely painted, grimacing Indian face surmounted by a bristling roach. Honey let out a terrified scream.

The dancers, frightened by her reaction, backed away hastily while the crowd let out a roar of approving laughter. "Honey, be sensible!" pleaded Margaret. "Our Indians don't capture and torture people any more! They're just like us!"

Honey did not hear her. Dixon, who had grabbed the postcard out of her hands and passed it to Evans, was shaking her by the shoulders. "It's a practical joke! The kid's played another trick on you!"

"Don't touch me! Ever!" she shrieked back at him. "You lied to me about Elsie! You made me believe she'd run away!" She struggled wildly to her unsteady feet to get away from him, knocking her glass off the table. Then slipping on an ice cube, she plunged to the floor.

Evans reached her first. "Come on, Mr. Dixon. Let's get her out of here and up to her room."

Arms around her, the two men followed by Margaret and Mary led her through the milling crowd.

Nearly two hours later Evans entered the sheriff's office to find Sheriff Mann and his deputy Shorty awaiting him with grim faces.

"I called you before noon, Mr. Evans," said Mann accusingly.

"I had a late lunch. Mrs. Wilbur suffered an upset."

"She's due for another one. You didn't hear the radio announcement of a murder in Gallup, then?"

Evans shook his head.

Mann passed him a typewritten sheet. "Here's a transcript."

Evans read swiftly:

... discovered this morning on the floor with a fatal stab wound in the chest. The Navajo has not yet been identified.

According to police authorities investigating the case, the rented court in which the body was found had been occupied by a Pueblo Indian and a small White girl. They have not been identified and their whereabouts are unknown.

To add further to the air of mystery surrounding the shocking murder, the proprietess of the court is reported to have found in the slain man's own quarters the dress allegedly worn by the child ...

"Do you suppose . . ." began Evans in a quiet voice.

"No!" said Mann. "I *know* that's our pair. Listen. Cerillos first reported that the child left the Plaza Wednesday evening with a Pueblo Indian. Baca saw her with him in Maria's lunchroom a short time later. Maria identified him as one Inocencio, and his

[70]

family confirmed to Shorty here that they stayed all night at their house near the pueblo. Now what happens? They vanish. But a car was stolen from the pueblo during the dance Thursday morning. The state police reports that the car was found abandoned just outside of Gallup. In it was a sack of those small clay animals made by the Indian's family for sale as souvenirs. And now comes this murder. And to back it all up, I telephoned Gallup this morning and got this description of the kid's dress found in the murdered Navvie's room." He shoved his scratch pad across the desk to Evans.

Evans silently slid back across the desk Elsie's postcard to her mother.

"That cinches it!" said the sheriff vehemently. "The Indian's probably murdered the girl, too, and stripped her of her clothes."

"I wouldn't assume that on circumstantial evidence, Mr. Mann," said Evans calmly.

"Hell no!" agreed Shorty. "They's something fishy about this whole affair. This postcard don't sound right. The old Indian ain't got enough sense to steal a car. He ain't done no kidnapping. This Inocencio's a worthless bottle-bit galoot, but he ain't no murderer. He wouldn't harm a flea if it was bitin' him you know where!"

"Anyway the city, county, and state authorities are going to back up my demand for a posse, to say nothing of the public when the news breaks," asserted Mann. "And guess who's going to head it—you, Shorty!"

"A posse? What for?" asked Shorty.

"To capture a murderer and kidnapper and a delinquent child if she's still alive!" shouted Mann. "This case has dragged on now for three days. Right during Fiesta when everybody in Hell's half-acre is here in Santa Fe to talk about it! What else do you expect me to do?"

"Seems like it's election year too," added Shorty. "You goin' to swear in the Injun Hater?"

"Damn it! The Indian Hater, as you call him, has served us as a valuable deputy on numerous occasions. No one else knows Indians better!"

"He jes' don't know people, thass all. But maybe Indians ain't people yet to some people. Look out he don't get you in no trouble."

"That's your lookout. You're headin' the posse, not me. Tomorrow morning!"

Evans leaned forward. "I must remind you I'm representing my client, Mrs. Wilbur, and will accompany the posse to Gallup. This seems to be a case involving many ramifications—allegations of a stolen car, kidnapping, murder. Two counties are also involved. But I want to make clear that Mrs. Wilbur's and my own chief concern is the safety and return of the child to her home."

All afternoon the old murderer and the delinquent child had been rolling steadily eastward in the Apache's creaking wagon. The team of broomtails, small and scrawny as they looked, was tough and tireless; they maintained a slow trot that kept the traces taut.

The Apache sat tall on the plank seat in a black sateen shirt and his new black hat whose high, round crown, not yet creased, stuck up like a length of stovepipe. Inocencio sat beside him, soft and shapeless in his faded red blanket. Behind in the empty wagon box jolted Elsie. Each time the wagon clattered down the slope of a rocky arroyo she clutched at the sideboards. When it leveled off again, she lay flat on a worn Navajo blanket to escape the dust. Her little bottom was sore, her thin back ached. She was hungry, tired and thirsty. The men in front never spoke nor looked back, and she suffered without complaint.

Sometime in the afternoon she dropped off to sleep. Awakening, she looked out with an anticipation that immediately changed to childish disappointment. The wagon seemed not to have moved at all. As far as she could see, the sunlit plain spread out empty and illimitable as before. There were the same deep arroyos slashed through the sage. The same red-rock buttes weirdly carved by wind and weather into lofty pinnacles and spires, great cathedrals, ships and sea shells. Far behind her two flat-topped mesas still rose pale lilac on the horizon. This was Indian Country. But where were they? A solitary horseman crossing a wash a mile away. A woman forlornly shepherding a tiny flock of sheep. That was all.

The little girl in her cowboy suit lay down again on her back to escape the dust and played with the toy pistol in her holster. Tiring of this, she folded her hands on her breast and lay staring up at the changing shapes of the white clouds gathering in the turquoise sky. "Now would be a good time to chew some bubble gum if I had any," she said aloud. "My mother isn't here." Neither of the Indians on the front seat spoke. The wagon kept moving on.

Late that afternoon the sweating broomtails puffed up the gradual slope of the foothills. The road forked: two wheel tracks continuing on, two more turning north. The Apache pulled up his team.

Inocencio clambered down from his seat. "We gettin' out," he said.

Elsie climbed out stiffly. The Apache slapped out his reins. As the team swung north, he flung up one arm in silent farewell. In a few minutes the wagon vanished over the rise.

"Where's he going, Inocencio?" the girl asked.

"Him Jicarilla."

"What's that?"

"Jicarilla Apache. This country belongin' to them Navajos."

[73]

Elsie looked around her with dismay. "But it looks all the same. I don't see any fences."

The old Indian strode off with his blanket roll without answering. The little girl trudged behind. Still the low hills sparsely covered with sage and piñon kept spreading out into an immense and rugged heartland that seemed to have no end at all. Scrambling to keep up with his long legs, the girl cried out, "Are we lost, Inocencio?"

"Not lost," he called back. "We gettin' there."

An hour later he lowered his roll and stopped to let her rest. Elsie dropped to the ground, taking off her new boots so she could wriggle her bare, tired feet in the sand.

Inocencio waited patiently. Then he shouldered his blanket roll again. "We goin 'now."

"But where, Inocencio?" the girl cried plaintively.

"Indian pueblo," he said shortly.

Envisioning a hot dinner and a comfortable bed with people like Pilar and Inocencio's old mother, Elsie scrambled to her feet and tucked her boots under one arm. They straggled on.

The sun was setting in a mass of darkening storm clouds when they reached the top of a low ridge and looked down into a desolate valley cut by a dry arroyo and flanked on one side by a wall of cliffs. There was no sign of life: no house, no man nor bird nor beast, not even a tree. There loomed only the spectral shape of a vast pile of crumbling masonry.

Tired, hungry, lonely and a little frightened, Elsie cried out in disappointment. "You said we were going to an Indian pueblo!"

"*Cómo no?* This Indian pueblo. Long time lots of peoples." He took her hand, and limping in her bare feet beside him, the girl trudged down toward the ruins.

Slowly it took shape before them under the scudding clouds: an immense walled city semi-circular in shape, its back wall once four stories high; a gigantic single building containing hundreds of rooms in the terraces surrounding its inner court.

"*Muy grande*! *Qué bonito*!" Inocencio said in a subdued voice, oppressed with veneration for the Old Ones.

"I don't think there's anything pretty about it!" said Elsie. "It's all fallen down! I'll bet nobody's lived here for a dozen years!"

"Long time," agreed Inocencio somberly.

Long before Marco Polo had journeyed to the court of Kublai Khan, five hundred years before Columbus had sailed to this old New World, it had stood here swarming with people at the crossroads of an ancient civilization. Looming out of the dark, prehistoric past, it still stood here, the first great building and the first great city in America, a metropolis deep in the desert heartland of a yet unknown continent. The storms of ten centuries had crumbled its walls, yet above it still hovered the dark wings of its high destiny.

Elsie shivered in the wan light. "It's kind of spooky, isn't it?"

The storm clouds were piling up now and the wind was whipping dust down the wash. Inocencio found some protection in a corner of two high walls; lowering his blanket roll, he went off to hunt for wood. Elsie wrapped up in one of the blankets, imitating him as she flipped it over her shoulders. She huddled down against the wall, idly trying to pry out one of the stones. The stones of Westminster Abbey had not yet been hewn when the stones in this strange old wall had been smoothed and set like mosaic, so perfectly fitted that they still held tight without mortar. Inocencio came back, built a fire, and put on meat and coffee.

Elsie watched him with a thoughtful face. Finally she asked, "Why did that man back there want to hurt me? I never did anything to him."

Inocencio stirred the fire without answering.

In a little while she asked haltingly, "Is he—he's dead, isn't he, Inocencio?"

"He dead."

The little girl shivered. "It's going to rain. I felt a drop right on my head. There's not even a roof on this old place."

Inocencio calmly turned over the meat.

Once again the girl broke out with a troubled question. "It isn't right, is it, Inocencio? Killing somebody, I mean."

"No good. Policemens don't like it."

"Well . . ."

The old Indian turned and looked at her with a dark and fathomless face. "I do it! What I has to do! I don't say nothin' more!" It was the voice of a man who had done what he had done and abided by it without regrets or excuses.

Elsie, however, still struggled childishly to link the past with the future. "Does that mean we can't EVER go home again? That I'll NEVER see my mother again?" Pathetically huddling against the wall from the drops of rain, she looked little like the arrogant child who had boasted proudly she would never go home. "But what will we do, Inocencio?"

Inocencio spoke firmly like a man who had long learned to live only in the existing moment. "We doin' what we do when we has to do it!" He got to his knees, lifted up the dripping mutton ribs. "Good meat! We eat him now!"

It was dark now, and they ate quickly under the spatter of raindrops. Inocencio stowed away his gear, slung the roll over his shoulder, and picked up a brand from the fire for a torch. Tripping over her dragging blanket, Elsie followed him into the dark, deserted city.

How weird it all was now—this vast honeycomb of empty cells through which she stumbled, following the flare of Inocencio's torch. He turned a corner far ahead of her and she was left in sudden, pitch blackness. Frantically trying to keep up, she tripped and fell headlong. She could not see his torch when she scrambled to her feet, but off to one side she glimpsed a length of wall lit by its pinkish flare. Across it moved the shadow of a cloaked monster. Soon there was another, smaller one running after it. They kept winding through a labyrinth of narrow passageways. *Zaguans,* plazas and rooms periodically outlined by flashes of sheet lightning.

The sky was suddenly rent by a jagged whiplash of fire. An instant later came the sharp crack of thunder followed by a roar reverberating with an ominous rumble. It was as if the gates of the storm had been cracked open—through them rushed a torrent of stinging rain. Inocencio stopped. Elsie had caught up with him and was jerking at the tail of his blanket.

"It rainin'," he said, looking down at her.

Elsie, too frightened to speak, pointed off to her right.

Inocencio raised his torch higher. From an open stretch of plaza protruded the top of a ladder. They walked toward it and stopped. Then testing its rungs, Inocencio slowly climbed down, followed by Elsie.

They found themselves now in a circular, subterranean room that looked to the girl at first glimpse like the inside of a big well. The hard-beaten earth floor was dry. The top—except for the ladder opening—was covered with logs and dirt. Inocencio, holding up the torch, was staring at the walls. They were covered with layers of colored pigment peeling away, each revealing queer symbols and figures of dancing men, birds and feathers painted in rich, faded colors.

"This old well's dry and it's got a roof," said Elsie, huddling down with relief.

"No well. It kiva."

Obviously it was one of the ancient, ceremonial kivas unearthed and partially restored by the archeological party mentioned by the trader back at the post. Inocencio remained standing with one

[77]

hand on the ladder, uneasy and anxious to climb back out of the sacred ceremonial chamber of the Old Ones.

"Mebbe go somewheres else," he said uneasily.

"Not me. I'm staying here where it's dry."

Elsie remained staring at the trickle of water coming through the roof opening and listening to the lash of the storm overhead. Reluctantly, Inocencio propped up his torch in the ancient fire-pit and unwrapped the blanket roll. Elsie took one of the dry blankets and wrapped it around her in imitation of Inocencio as he squatted down.

"What's a kiva?" she asked.

Inocencio looked at her with a curious expression on his dark, wrinkled face. It was the seed-pattern of the whole multiworld universe itself. In the floor at the girl's feet was a little hole: the *sipapu*, leading down into the first underworld, the Place of Beginning whence came man. The floor level, circular as the earth when glimpsed from a midpoint, was the second world into which man emerged. Around the wall still stood remnants of a seating ledge, representing the third world which opened through the roof to the fourth world of man's successive existences. Overhead stretched the great hand-hewn viga or roof-beam; the Beam-Above-the-Earth, the immortal Galaxy in the sky above, leading toward the world existences yet to come. Through them all, from the fire-pit to the altar place, ran mankind's Road of Life upon which centuries ago men had danced here the ceremonial recapitulation of their long evolutionary journey . . . And yet if the kiva was the symbol of the macrocosmic vastness of the universe, it also symbolized the microcosmic womb in which man had developed. For to these men of a new race on a new and unknown continent, the whole universe was contained within the Mother of Creation, within man himself . . . Inocencio and the wordless forefathers of his race had no way nor need to explain all this. They had only to look about them here to see the architectural form of their vast

[78]

cosmological universe; and to know that it was duplicated within their own bodies, each a fleshly kiva, a living universe, as the psychical soul form of all creation. It was all here, form and faith, expressed simply as an abstract and archetypal symbol.

"I said what's a kiva?" Elsie repeated in a petulant voice.

"It Indian church."

"But it doesn't look like a church to me!" persisted the child.

"White people's church stick up in sky pointin' at White people's Heaven. Indian church go down deep in belly of Our Mother Earth. We no forget she borns us. She give us ever'thing good we got."

The old Indian's voice was curt. He drew his blanket up over his face. Plainly he did not want to talk about such matters.

Elsie sat staring at the mural designs in the flickering flare of the torch. The queer-looking men reminded her of the masked dancers she had seen in the plaza of the pueblo. There were lots of birds, too. All in a soft, muted patina. But so strange, everything.

"Well, anyway, it's got some pretty pictures." She twisted her head around to follow a queer figure that ran like a motif around the room. "What's that funny snake with wings on like a bird? There isn't any such thing!"

"You keepin' quiet!" warned Inocencio darkly. "Him got the power of the earth and the sky, too. Long time the Old Ones paint him on them big rocks at home. Pilar put him on her potteries, too. He got the power all right. *Awanyu.* That his name. You be polite!"

The torch was beginning to burn out. Its red flare barely lighted their faces. Both that of the child and the old Indian showed that they were deeply conscious in their own ways of the other-dimensional functions for which this ancient, sacred chamber was built. The rain kept trickling down the pole ladder.

Elsie, like any inquisitive child, could not forbear asking forthrightly, "But I saw you kneeling in church that morning, Inocen-

[79]

cio. You say your prayers, too. I thought you believed in God, not idols."

The old Indian looked annoyed. This matter of why he believed in the power of *Awanyu*, and of God, too, was too complex for his simple mind. "It everywhere, in earth and sky and trees and rocks —everything. White peoples think they close him up in church like jail."

The torch suddenly burned out, leaving them in darkness. Still, a moment later, Elsie's voice sounded again. "But Inocencio . . . "

"No!" The old Indian's voice was stubborn. "I not talkin' about them things! I sleepin'!"

Above them, like the disembodied kachina forces of generations of storms, the wind and the rain prowled through the ruins of the ancient city.

E arlier that evening Evans had returned to Honey's hotel suite. Margaret was already there, reading in a chair beside her, like Dixon. Honey was lying outstretched on the sofa. Her face, devoid of rouge and lipstick, was white and calm above her dark brown dressing gown. Only her hair—that wonderful honeyed growth which was the pride of everyone who knew her—spread loosely alive over the pillows, shimmering with the immense, youthful vitality that made her so beautiful.

That noon, after her breakdown in the cantina, they had led her, drunk and hysterical, to her suite, then put her to bed, given her a sedative. Yet at sunset Honey had roused to demand that Mary give her a hot bath and a shampoo. "If only my hair is washed, I'll begin to feel better," she kept insisting. This was the only touch of vanity Honey had ever betrayed to Evans' knowledge. Yet it reminded him of how Pueblo Indians always washed their hair carefully in yucca suds before participating in a sacred ritual. "It bring the life up," an old medicine-man once had told him. So now after a cup of tea she lay quietly, calm and sober.

She greeted Evans warmly, without rising. "What a nuisance I was to you this noon," she said. "I was drunk and obstreperous. Martinis, Elsie's postcard, and those Indians were too much for me. Is there any more news?"

Evans spread out a late edition of the paper with the bold-face headline:

MISSING GIRL FEARED
INDIAN KIDNAP VICTIM

City police, the sheriff's office, and New Mexico State Police are pushing their search for small Elsie Wilbur, now believed to have been kidnapped by a depraved Indian from Tewa Pueblo.

The brutal murder of a Navajo in a squalid court in Gallup where the two have been traced, and the discovery of the child's dress, arouse fears for her safety. There is yet no clue as to where the murderer may have fled with her, or if she is still alive, but a posse is being formed to track him . . .

Summoning courage for an unpleasant task, he rose and carried the paper to Honey. She sat up, spreading it out so Margaret could read it, too.

"Before you read it, I must remind you that we can't depend on newspaper scareheads. They're always prone to sensationalism," he said calmly. "I've talked with Sheriff Mann and Shorty. They're organizing a posse to pursue the search for Elsie. Certainly the facts warrant a full investigation, and I will accompany them tomorrow morning."

Dixon was the first to speak after he too had read the reportage. "I'm sorry, dear."

"I'm sorry, too, Freddie. But it's broken the relationship between us. I believed you when you said Elsie had just run away again. Now I see something else has happened. So just pack up your things and leave quietly. I'm in no shape to stand another unpleasant scene."

Evans felt a sudden rush of respect for her. It had been a difficult decision for her to make; he had suspected all too easily the physical attraction that held this beautiful, vital, and lonely woman to a man as charming and talented as Dixon. Yet the absence of all feeling in her voice showed him how completely she meant it.

Unembarrassed, Dixon was as calm and resolute as Honey. "This is not the time and place to talk about it. Nor are you in any condition to. There's only one thing I want to say. Elsie will be found safe and well. But she'll still be a problem child you can't cope with alone. You'll need the support of a man who loves you as I do, Honey. Make no mistake about that! I'll begin to assume my share of responsibility tomorrow morning if Mr. Evans will permit me to accompany him and the posse."

If Evans on their first meeting might have suspected Dixon of being one of those vapid and irresponsible lovers so many rich American women pick up in Europe, he had now changed his mind. No, Dixon was no quitter. He could assert himself; he had a mind of his own. And he needed it with a woman as strong-willed as Honey, however things turned out.

"I'll be glad to have you come along with me," Evans answered, standing up and motioning to Margaret. "Now we must be going so as to get an early start. I'll keep you informed by telephone of all developments, Mrs. Wilbur."

Honey also rose. "You expect me to sit here, then, while strangers are searching for my own child?"

"It's the only sensible thing to do, dear," said Margaret walking to the door.

Honey did not reply. But as Evans and Margaret stepped out into the hall, she turned to Dixon standing beside her. "How strange it is after all this time, and all our love-making, we've never got acquainted!"

Entering the elevator, Margaret shuddered at the cold cruelty of her remark.

Early next morning the deputies sworn in for Shorty's posse were gathering in front of the County Court House. The deserted street and empty Plaza beyond wore the forlorn look of utter exhaustion: gutters were choked with confetti, paper bags, and tamale husks; art displays had been removed; torn lengths of colored streamers were strewn on the grass-grown flagstones; even the "Portal Tribe" had abandoned the Palace. The bells of Saint Francis Cathedral were ringing for early Sunday Mass in voices muted, tired and *muy triste*. All illusions evoked by Fiesta had vanished, and the roughly dressed, booted, and armed men created a jarring aspect of reality.

Shorty, impatiently walking back and forth in front of the window from which Sheriff Mann and Dixon were peering out, yanked his big Ingersoll out of his vest pocket. "Whar in the hell's the Injun Hater?" he exclaimed in exasperation. "Ever' time some pore Red S. O. B. goes off'n the track, he's itchin' to take out them dogs and that thirty-thirty!"

"Oh, Jack Smith ain't so bad except he hates all Indians like poison," said one of the men. "Can't say I blame him too much. That was a nice ranch of his the Gover'ment give to them Tewas."

"He knows them. You got to admit that, Shorty," said another. "And for smellin' out this murderin' kidnapper he's just what the doctor ordered."

[83]

A weathered, mud-splattered station wagon drove up to the curb, its back filled with a pack of sad-eyed hunting dogs. The driver—Jack Smith, the Indian Hater—got out and walked toward the men, carrying a .30–.30 caliber rifle with a worn stock. He was an old, white-headed, hawk-faced man with an embittered expression and wearing an ancient, bloodstained, fringed buckskin jacket and moccasin boots. A lingering old-timer of harder days, he was a character to all who knew him and his one obsession. Years ago he had filed on a fair spread of mesa. But hardly had he built up his ranch before federal court action finally restored it to Tewa Pueblo with all the land originally granted it by the Crown of Spain. Due settlement was made to him, but the bitterness of his loss developed into a psychopathic hatred of his Indian successors. Periodically he tore down their fences, ran off their stock, and burned their crops. Finally restrained, the Indian Hater nursed his reputation by serving as a deputy sheriff on infrequent occasions when erring Indians and stolen stock needed tracking down. No one liked him, but everyone admitted his competence.

Now jumping lightly to the curb, he shouted, "Let's git goin' after that murderin' child attacker! Me and the dogs are itchin' to git after him!" He patted the rifle in the crook of his left arm.

Shorty's small, stocky body stiffened. "I'm runnin' this here party, Mister. When you put this on, you're takin' orders from me!" He flipped a deputy's badge at the Indian Hater, who avidly pinned it on his greasy buckskin jacket. "Nothin's been proved on this Inocencio yet. That's fer the court to decide. We jes' aim to find him and the kid and bring 'em back. Savvy?"

The old Indian Hater lifted his rifle and squinted through its telescopic sights. "Old Hawk-Eye'll find him, son!"

With a sweep of his hand Shorty knocked the rifle off the imaginary target. The Indian Hater whirled on him, his rheumy blue eyes blazing. Shorty bellied up to him with cold, restrained anger.

"You play any quick-shootin' tricks in my posse, Injun Hater, and I'll tear that stringy white scalp off'n yer head with my bare hands! Savvy?"

The old man backed away, grumbling.

"Oh, cut it out!" yelled one of the posse. "This ain't goin' to be no picnic without your fussin' at each other!"

As the men began to pile into the station wagon and another car, Evans drove up to the curb in his big touring sedan. In the back seat sat Margaret and Honey, who had insisted on coming as they had known she would. For a moment Evans watched the roughly dressed deputies scrambling for seats in the other two cars. Then Dixon appeared, looking out of place in his English herringbone tweed jacket and flannel trousers. Evans opened the car door and leaned out.

"Freddie! I've been expecting you! Come and ride up here with me!"

Neither of the women spoke as Dixon gratefully crawled into the front seat beside Evans.

"Keep in touch! Hear!" shouted Sheriff Mann from the curb as the three cars drove off.

The pursuit had begun.

Innocencio and Elsie stood under a big pine in a growth of brush, staring out hungrily at a small ranch in the clearing. They had finally climbed out of Indian country and reached the lower slopes of the mountains. It was cattle range: rough plateaus covered with piñon and chaparral, sparsely dotted with pines, and opening out upon *vegas* where straggles of Herefords and occasional bands of broomtail horses grazed upon the sere brown grass. There were few ranches in this remote area, often isolated by impassable roads, between the Jicarilla Apache Reservation and the little Spanish villages in the high blue range marking the Continental Divide. The ranch before them looked no different from the rest: a small log cabin whose walls were chinked with adobe, a big log barn, and a dilapidated corral of weathered aspen poles from which the bark was peeling. Inocencio grunted with satisfaction. It was mid-morning, the place seemed deserted, although a faint wisp of smoke was rising out of the chimney.

"Don't see no pickup around. Mebbe them ranch people gone off somewhere." He let down his blanket roll and pushed Elsie back a little farther in the brush. "You stayin' here." He walked out into the clearing. The girl watched him approach the house warily, peer in the open door, then slide around the corner out of sight.

The side window was open. The old Indian, standing on his toes, cautiously peeked inside. The kitchen was sparsely furnished and unoccupied. A fire was still burning in the wood-stove against the far wall. In the corner was a stand on which sat a water bucket and tin dipper. The table in the center of the room was cluttered with dirty dishes. The old man, eagerly sniffing the warm fragrant air, was not satisfied. He raised still higher on his toes to glimpse on the table just below the window four fresh loaves of bread that the ranchwoman evidently had taken out of the oven before leaving.

For a minute or two Inocencio watched and listened. Then stealthily he reached both hands inside, picked up a loaf of the fresh bread, and stowed it carefully inside his blanket. Licking his lips, he was too occupied to see a sturdy middle-aged woman who appeared in the doorway across the room as he continued to stow loaves in his blanket. She halted abruptly at the astounding sight that met her eyes: two brawny, dark brown hands reaching over the window sill, groping over the table, and picking up the last loaf of her steaming hot bread.

[86]

The woman's resolute face hardened; she had lived here a long time. Quietly she picked up a broom and tiptoed across the room to the kitchen door. Raising her weapon, she opened the screen door and stepped outside just as Inocencio, with the stolen bread bundled up in his blanket, crept round the corner. Instantly, she brought the head of the broom down on Inocencio's head with a resounding whop. He flung up an arm to protect himself, and a loaf of bread tumbled out of his blanket. She whacked him again, and another loaf went rolling on the ground.

"You thievin' Indian! Stealin' my bread! I'll learn you!"

Elsie, watching from the brush, could see it all. Convulsed with laughter, she childishly jumped up and down, clapping her hands in excitement.

The ludicrous spectacle of the big Indian being abjectly buffeted by the ranchwoman hopping about him and wielding her broom, the loaves of bread tumbling in all directions, came to a sudden climax when Inocencio's legs became entangled in his blanket and he fell sprawling on the ground.

He scrambled to his feet, grabbing up a loaf of bread. With this single prize clutched tightly under his arm, he fled across the clearing toward Elsie with the ranchwoman in pursuit. The woman finally became winded; giving up the chase, she walked back to the house.

Elsie was still laughing when Inocencio reached her. "She hit you with her broom, didn't she? And you didn't hit her back, either!"

Inocencio's pride was hurt. He drew himself up in all his dignity, then slipped aside the edge of his blanket to reveal his captured prize. Elsie stopped laughing at the sight of the warm brown loaf.

"Ai. Ai. Ai. I got him!" the old Indian said proudly, thrusting the loaf at her. Taking up his blanket roll with one hand, and grabbing her with the other, he fled with her into the patch of forest.

[87]

At the far edge they paused to rest. Munching a slice of bread apiece, they peered out at a small band of horses grazing and sleepily whisking flies.

"We're going to have another slice, aren't we? Wish we had some strawberry jam to put on it," said Elsie wistfully.

Inocencio wrapped up the bread without replying, and continued to study the horses carefully. After a long time he stood up. "You keepin' quiet," he ordered her softly.

The little girl in the cowboy suit watched him walk slowly out into the open and stop. She knew how horses ought to be caught; she had watched movie cowboys lots of times. One ran out recklessly among the snorting, prancing horses, whirling the loop of his lariat. It always settled neatly, at the first throw, over the head of the big, proud stallion. As the horse bolted, the cowboy dug in the high heels of his boots for the battle that always made her spill her popcorn in excitement. The strong, handsome cowboy always won. Hand by hand he pulled himself up on the taut rope to the wildly plunging stallion, then leaped on bareback to show how unafraid he was.

The old Indian did not act brave at all. For a moment Elsie even doubted his intention; he didn't have a rope to whirl. Big and pudgy-looking in his blanket, he just stood there motionless until the horses saw and smelled him. Then very slowly and unconcernedly he moved a little closer and stopped again.

Only Inocencio could muster such care and patience. He acted as if he had all day, and seemed interested in everything but the horses. Whenever one of them threw up a head suspiciously and looked as if he might spook and run off, the old Indian walked away and stood looking out across the plain. Maybe he chewed on a blade of grass for a little while. When the band resumed grazing, he moved up closer.

All the time now Elsie could hear him talking in his soft, singsong Indian voice. It sounded so soothing and monotonous she was suddenly surprised to see that he was among the horses. Scratching one on the rump, stroking another's flank, still talking. But never putting out his hand to the head, and paying no attention at all to a well-coupled, nervous little white mare watching him suspiciously. In fact, he turned his back toward her to talk to and stroke a big, rawboned bay horse. Everything he did now was in slow motion, hands held up and moving so slowly they didn't seem to move at all. Working around the bay until he was close to the white mare, he gently slid his left hand under her neck and deftly reached his right hand over her shoulder out of sight. The mare drew back, and Elsie saw that Inocencio had slipped around her a piece of rope that he had concealed in the folds of his blanket. It was done.

He took his time now making a crude hackamore. When it was knotted, he put his hand on her mane and lightly for a man so old and big, jumped astride her. The mare wheeled sideways, trying to get her head down and heels up, then bolted across the plain, spooking all the rest of the band. This was the battle Elsie wanted to see! Yet even now Inocencio was in no hurry. He had no will to dominate. He simply sat easily on her back and let her run, gradually turning her back to Elsie.

He pulled her up gently, and looking down said quietly, "Cowboy got to have horse. Good one!"

Elsie handed up the blanket roll for him to balance across his lap. Then he pulled her up to sit behind him, and shook the strong little mare into a slow trot.

All day they kept climbing into the slowly rising mountains. How beautiful they were after the desolate stretches of sage and sand: big ridges of pine forest, the thick growth of piñon, clear little streams, and more and more often a dark, deep canyon in which the air was cool and fresh. Ahead of them a tiny white spot

[89]

kept growing into a bold escarpment of white cliffs. No matter which way they went for easier riding, Inocencio eventually turned the mare back toward it.

Riding a horse was a new experience for Elsie; she felt like a real cowboy in her suit. There was a sensuous pleasure in feeling the smooth, rhythmic working of the muscles underneath her, the body heat rising from the mare's flanks as she labored with snorting breaths up a steep slope. Then how loose and relaxed she was when she plunged down the grade and broke into a trot. Elsie, shaken and panting, listening to the rattle of stones thrown up by the hooves behind her, could still gasp out with pleasurable excitement, "We've taken the brakes off! Haven't we, Inocencio!"

The old Indian did not answer. He pulled up the mare, and again she resumed her slow, plodding climb.

The little girl could feel Inocencio the same way she felt the horse, as for the first time she began to know him with a strange physical intimacy. How big he was! His massive body rose up in front of her like a stout pillar to which she clung for support. Always wrapped in his blanket, with his hair braids hanging down, he somehow looked soft and womanly. Now that she held him, she could feel the strength inside. Grasping his shoulders, she felt his full neck sloping down to his heavy shoulders and broad back. Most of the time she held him around the waist. Then she felt the muscles in his sides and belly rhythmically tightening and loosening with the gait of the mare and his slow, deep breathing. Even when she hooked her hands into his big belt, she could feel the stringy little muscles in his pliant waist. There was nothing soft about Inocencio! Nor did he bulge with muscles like a circus strong man. He was softly rounded all over, but stout and firm as the little mare beneath them. The sense of his solidity gave the girl a comforting feeling of security. He felt just like she used to imagine her father would feel if she could crawl into his lap, but he was always away or too busy or something. So she leaned against Inocencio, nestled her head against his wide back, and hugged him tight.

Inocencio paid no attention to her at all. He just kept the mare climbing. After awhile nothing was any fun at all. Her short legs grew cramped from straddling the plump mare; her arms ached from hanging on to Inocencio; her bottom became numb from bouncing up and down and then it began to get sore. She tried sitting sideways, then turned the other way. More and more often she slid off whenever Inocencio stopped to let the mare catch breath, and lay flat on her belly.

"I guess I'm getting tired where I sit down," she said without complaining.

The old Indian looked at her pinched mouth and the circles forming under her eyes, then stared at the rampart of white cliffs looming up the canyon.

"Cowboy don't get tired ridin' no horse," he said. But this time he pulled her up where he could hold her in front of him.

Elsie lay back against him, grasping the arm around her, listening to his heart thumping in his big chest. The mare was getting wet now, and Elsie could feel the sweat soaking through the legs and seat of her pants. It had a warm, horsey smell new to her. She also began to notice that Inocencio had a peculiar body odor of his own. It was an Indian smell, rather spicy, that wasn't unpleasant at all; it smelled just like him.

Late that afternoon Inocencio pulled up the mare on a low ridge sticking out like a tongue from the mouth of the canyon. They both got off. Inocencio removed the hackamore from the mare and gave her a swat on the rump. The freed mare whirled away, stopped and looked back as if expecting them to chase her. Then nibbling mouthfuls of grass, she began to make her way back down the slope.

"We done ridin'. She goin' home now," said Inocencio.

The little white mare had become so familiar that Elsie hated to see her go, tired of riding as she was. "But where are we going, Inocencio? Down there?" She pointed down off the ridge to her right at a straggle of adobes: one of the small, ancient Spanish villages that had existed in these mountains, half-hidden and almost forgotten, since Colonial-Spanish days. "What's that town? Is that where we're going?"

"El Zaguan they call that *pueblocito.*"

"Why does it have that funny name?"

"That a place goin' through wall from one place to another place," Inocencio answered, helplessly trying to define the passageway through a wall between two patios or *placitas.* "You see him there." He nodded toward the escarpment of white rock to his left. Elsie saw now that it marked a steep, narrow canyon cleft through the high mountain wall—the defile which had given the village its name. "That the *zaguan* where we goin'," he said curtly, picking up the blanket roll.

The little girl without a protest followed him down the ridge away from the village.

The sun was setting when they reached the mouth of the canyon at the bottom of the pass. The old Indian stopped and looked carefully about him. The secluded mountain glade, beautiful in its virginal serenity, was a lawn of green velvet surrounded by tall pines. Through it dashed a sparkling stream from a waterfall at the upper end. On each side the walls were banked with columbines and tall, lacy ferns.

"Good place!" grunted Inocencio, putting down his pack.

Elsie, suddenly frightened by a harsh, raucous sound, drew up close to him. "What's that?"

Inocencio calmly nodded toward a large black and white bird scolding them from a nearby tree. "Him magpie."

In the lengthening shadows he gathered wood, built a fire. On

[92]

the ground in front of a big boulder he piled branches of fir; over these he spread their blankets. Elsie had never camped out before. "We're not going to stay here, are we?" she asked anxiously. "All night long, Inocencio? There's no house!"

"Best house in whole world!" the old Indian assured her confidently. He looked up at the sky. "Got good roof." He nodded at the pile of soft fir tips covered with blankets, and then at the fire. "Good bed. Good stove. Got everything!"

"But we don't have anything to eat, Inocencio!" The bedraggled little cowboy, exhausted from riding all day, was almost to the point of tears.

Inocencio calmly set out coffee, salt, sugar, and the remaining bread. He bolted together the stock and barrel of the twenty-two rifle he had bought at the trading post, slipped some shells in the magazine. Standing up, he let fall his blanket. "Go get supper now. Cowboy stayin' right here. Don't movin'." He vanished among the pines.

The little girl huddled close to the fire, wrapping herself in a blanket. Still she shivered apprehensively, staring into the darkening woods. Suddenly there sounded a shot. She jumped to her feet, peering toward the sound. In a little while Inocencio reappeared. He was carrying a cottontail, already skinned and cleaned.

In silence and the gathering dusk he put the rabbit on to broil, filled the coffee pot, broke the bread. They ate, wiping their fingers on their hair braids. Then Inocencio brought out from its hiding place in his bedroll one of the lollipops the trader had given him. With it greedily stuffed in her mouth, Elsie looked more natural.

"I've got a sucker! It's a 'Pink Puppy' one, too! Now don't you wish you had a little drink of whiskey?" For the first time there was no derision in her voice. Her face showed a look of solicitude, a hint of comradeship Inocencio had not seen before. His own face set in a kind expression of paternal care.

[93]

"Good mountain water. Better than whiskey, I think," he lied, licking his lips almost imperceptively. "Now we go sleep, I say."

He led her to the bed of soft fir needles, tucked the blankets around her. Then he went back to sit wrapped in his own blanket in front of the fire at her feet.

It was dark now. The fire died. The wind soughed in the pines. The stream rippled noisily over the rocks.

"Aren't you going to sleep here, too, Inocencio?" the girl asked sleepily. "Mother never let me sleep with her. She was always sleeping with my father or Freddie or somebody else, I guess, and never wanted me. Sometimes Mary let me get in bed with her in the morning, but she always had to get up when the bell rang for Mother's coffee just when I was getting warm and comfy."

"I sleepin' right here. Same as always." Inocencio's voice was kind but gruff.

"Well then, move up here closer where I can touch you with my feet, won't you Inocencio? Just in case somebody or a bear tries to hurt me."

"I don't let nothin' hurt you! I watchin'!" Nevertheless, he moved up close to her feet. For a long time he sat somberly staring into the coals. In the dying red glow Elsie was lying quiet and relaxed. Stealthily, he reached a hand under the edge of her blankets, tenderly taking off one of her little cowboy boots and then the other. The girl let out a deep sigh and straightened out in sleep.

T̶he Evans party, following the posse from Santa Fe, drove into Gallup late in the afternoon. Evans and Margaret, with Honey and Dixon, checked into the old Fred Harvey hotel, El Navajo. When the two women were comfortably settled in their rooms, Evans and Dixon left to meet with the posse. Then they picked up Shorty to accompany them for a talk with the local police authorities.

Their attitude depressed Evans. It was unfortunate, he thought, that the murder in which his client's child was involved had taken place in Gallup. The plight of the Navajos in this trading center had been a disgrace for years. There was no escaping the fact that all the drunken and debauched Navajos on the Reservation made of Railroad Avenue and Sand Flat a horror that rivaled any big-city slum. It was equally undeniable that they were preyed upon by white bootleggers, peyote and marijuana vendors, and town bullies who frequently clubbed them at night, stripped them of their silver jewelry, and left them lying in the gutter or railroad yards. One had only to glimpse the jail packed with impounded Navajos unable to speak English or to understand what had befallen them, destitute of money to pay their fines, and without any help or protection whatever, to realize the grievous imbalance between Indian and White on this modern frontier. Nobody admitted it because nobody knew what to do about it, but it lay heavily on the social conscience.

This shocking murder on Sand Flat, with fear for the kidnapped little White girl, had brought it all to surface in a rash of hysterical publicity. In the angry outcries Evans could detect a righteous justification of the inherent White antipathy toward Indians. People demanded a scapegoat. It made no difference that Inocencio was from a peaceful, neighboring pueblo and was, as Shorty stoutly affirmed, a harmless old man. The aroused public already had convicted him of depravity, kidnapping, and murder; and the authorities readily assented to the outcry against him.

When Evans and Dixon did not return for dinner, Margaret ate alone at the horseshoe lunch counter, telephoned her children and their baby-sitter, and went to her room to read. Honey, indisposed, ordered a tray sent up to her own room.

[95]

Later that evening the two men returned to the hotel and telephoned the two women to meet them in the lobby. Evans briefly outlined the situation. The posse from Santa Fe County would be joined in the morning by several deputies from McKinley County. There were no clues as to which way Inocencio and Elsie may have gone. Due south lay Zuni Pueblo, the largest in New Mexico, where they certainly would be recognized. The main highway west, heavily traveled, led through Arizona to California. Hence the decision was made that the posse would drive north into the Navajo Reservation and stop at trading posts along the way.

"I'll be ready to leave at any time," said Honey.

Evans protested. "It was my understanding that you and Margaret were coming only this far. The search obviously will be long and tiring. There are no accommodations and eating facilities. This is a comfortable hotel. You'll be better off waiting here. I'm thinking of my wife as well as you. She came only to keep you company."

"I'd have stayed in Santa Fe if I wanted to wait and be comfortable. I want to find my child."

"I realize your concern," Evans said drily, "but you can't be of any help and you might hinder the men."

"Elsie's my daughter! Wherever she's gone, I'm going!"

Evans rose, unable to persuade her. "You may thank Margaret for agreeing to accompany you."

Dixon followed Honey to the door of her room. "Can I do anything for, Honey?"

"Yes, if you've a mind to. Find me a drink of Scotch in this Sunday-dry town to settle my nerves and put me to sleep!"

The pale dove-gray light of dawn was seeping through the pine tips when Inocencio shook Elsie awake, putting a hand over her mouth and beckoning. The girl scrambled into her boots and stealthily followed him down toward the stream. At first she could not see it standing over a still trout pool. Then slowly the antlers lifted, the petals of its ears twitched; she glimpsed the big soft eyes, the sloping shoulders and long, narrow forelegs.

"It's a deer! A real live deer!" the girl shouted excitedly, clapping her hands. "Just like the little clay one I lost!"

With one twitch of its tail piece, the deer bounded swiftly away as a gray ghost.

The old Indian and the girl walked back to camp. Kindling the morning fire, he asked, "You got pin?"

The little girl undid her cowboy pants with childish modesty and took out a small safety pin from her panties. "It's one of the little gold ones Mother got in Paris. You better not lose it."

Inocencio was unimpressed. "Too shiny. I fix him just the same," he grumbled. Laboriously, he fashioned it into a hook. "You makin' too much noise. Stayin' here now." He walked away.

Elsie knelt feeding little twigs to the flames. The fire was hungry as she was; it ate them up fast, even snapping at her fingers. Tiring of this, she squatted back on her haunches and watched the sun come up over the pines and listened to the birds. She was quiet so long that a rabbit hopped into sight. It stopped on seeing her, putting its long ears forward and moving its nose in funny little twitches. Elsie put out her hand, but there was a sudden snap of twigs and the rabbit hopped away. The girl flung around to see Inocencio approaching.

"I saw a rabbit, too! He wiggled his ears at me!"

"*Cómo no?*" Inocencio held up a string of rainbow trout. "Our Mother Earth give us all the good things we got. We not forgettin'."

He picked up a small burning twig and blew a tuft of smoke to each of the directions: to the east, the south, west, and north, to the four worlds symbolized by the elements that gave him life, the fire, the air, the waters, and the earth. Nor did he forget the Below, the Place of Beginning, and the Above where man had still to go. "We eatin' breakfast now," he said complacently, unsheathing his knife.

Elsie watched him slit each trout down the belly, deftly scrape out the insides. There were some thin slices from the bacon slab he had saved for grease, a piece of bread, and coffee.

"Ai. Ai Ai. We got everything!"

They ate quietly in the sunlight flooding the glade. Then Inocencio got up. "Good world! Nothin' spoiled. I showin' you."

They walked slowly into the forest on a carpet of fallen needles. The great pines drew aside to form a high, vaulted nave gilded with early morning sunlight. It reminded Elsie of that big cathedral in France or Germany or somewhere to which her mother had taken her, and she believed she had seen, high above the sanctuary, the clear, pale sheen of the Pearly Gates. But this great nave arched up to Heaven so high and was so luminously gilded that the girl stared upward half-believing that the light was reflected from no less than the Golden Throne itself. The solemnity of an eerie peace enfolded her. She forgot her stiff legs and sore bottom in the mystery of its unearthly beauty. She took Inocencio's hand, and they walked on in silence.

The posse was just leaving Gallup: Shorty's deputies from Santa Fe, more armed deputies from McKinley County, the station wagon containing the Indian Hater and his dogs, and Evans' big car following behind.

Evans drove with a worried frown. Dixon sat beside him, freshly shaven and nervous. Honey and Margaret sat quietly in back with a box lunch and a flask of cognac on the seat beside them, staring silently out the window as the car rolled across Railroad Avenue and headed north into the Navajo Reservation.

Flat, treeless and appallingly empty, the high sage plain kept spreading out. A solitary weathered building appeared, and a half-hour later, another. Some of the men went in each one, came out shaking their heads, and the cars drove on. Abruptly, the cars were stopped by a flock of sheep. An old Navajo, his gray hair tied with a purple headband, was patiently watching the packed, bleating sheep ebbing slowly as water across the road.

"What's the matter with that old man?" exclaimed Honey irritably. She jumped up, leaned over the front seat between Evans and Dixon, and imperiously sounded the horn.

Margaret caught her wrist. "Dear! He can't help it! I know how you feel. But please don't be impatient."

The old Navajo, back toward them, continued watching his sheep without turning around.

In back of the next trading post stood a clump of cottonwoods. The men got out to sprawl in the shade and eat. The Evans party stayed in their car, eating their box lunch and sipping coffee from the thermos with a spot of cognac, and watching the Indian Hater walk his dogs. A strange, tense picnic lunch.

Early that afternoon the cars drew up in front of still another post, a massive fortress of rock and adobe on the naked plain. In a little while Shorty, the Indian Hater and two deputies came out the door talking and gesturing excitedly.

"Good news fer you, Ma'am!" announced Shorty. "They was here last Sattiday!"

"My baby! She's—"

"Frisky as a colt, Ma'am! Kickin' up her heels in new boots!"

"Thank God! She's alive and safe, Margaret! Did you hear?"

The news that they had picked up the fugitives' trail at last, and that Elsie was still alive and unharmed, broke the tension for them all. Yet as Evans joined the men crowding around Shorty and the Indian Hater, he was oppressed again by misgivings.

"I told you boys we'd git wind of the thievin' murderer up this way!" broke out the Indian Hater boastfully, squirting out a

[99]

stream of tobacco juice. "An Injun allays heads fer Injun country, not fer no big towns."

"Which way you reckon he's headin' now?" asked one of the deputies. "The trader never seen him leave."

"Let's go on to the next post," suggested one. "Maybe we can pick up some more information."

Another deputy suggested, "My guess is that they're clearing out of the state. Why don't we drive on to the Colorado line?"

The Indian Hater stood staring contemptuously at them without answering.

"Have yer say, Injun Hater. That's what yer here for," Shorty said curtly.

The Indian Hater spat derisively on the ground at their feet. "Yer thinkin' like White men. I knowed you would. Now a White man would head out of the country as fur as he could git. But an Injun . . ."

"Cut out the preachin'!" demanded Shorty. "This ain't no Sunday School!"

The Indian Hater spat again. "I know a Pueblo Injun, son! He allays heads fer his home mountains. Fer the piece of ole Mother Earth what suckled him and his folks. He figures he'll be safe in her arms . . . That's what he feels. He jes' can't hep hisself."

His forceful logic prohibited any arguments. To emphasize it, the Indian Hater flung out his arm toward the wheel tracks winding through the sage toward the rising blue mountains.

"There's his range, boys! Don't fergit he's got hisself a gun!" He patted his own ever present rifle.

"O.K." said Shorty. "I know that road. It goes up toward the Jicarilla Apache country and swings off by that old spread of Joe Jenkins. We'll mosey up that way and see if we can pick up any tracks, and check in at the ranch house . . . I'll ride with you, Injun Hater. Just in case you work yerself into a mild case of hurry."

The men began piling into their cars.

[100]

Evans turned to Honey. "This is too distressing for you, Mrs. Wilbur. Now that they've picked up the trail, I suggest we turn back to Gallup and wait developments. It's going to be rough and slow traveling."

"Turn back when I know my baby is alive and needs me? Never! Not if I have to ride with the Indian Hater and his dogs!"

"All right," said Margaret with a look at Evans. "We'll go a bit farther."

The station wagon and the cars drove off slowly, the men leaning out to catch sight of any footprints.

Hand in hand the old Indian and the little White girl walked down the nave of the great forest cathedral on a carpet of pine needles and entered a world that was old when this one was young, a world that would still be young when this one would be old and worn and weary. This was more than a single day they spent together feeling safe from pursuit and lost to the stark reality of their tragic flight. Always for Elsie it would preserve the strange and tenuous dimension of a timeless interlude that nothing could ever touch, as she remembered being shown by an old Indian the secrets of its wild and pristine beauty. For Inocencio, too, the day held all the mystery of a supreme adventure whose intangible components he had no mind to perceive. He had never had a child of his own, and the children of his pueblo had shunned him and his bottle. Now at last he was awakened to the paternal pride of responsibility and the joy of sacrifice. Always he had nursed an unconscious fear and hatred of Whites; a racial barrier through which, with this small White girl, he had finally broken to their common humanness. What he had to show her were more than the secrets of his world of nature. They were the priceless jewels of his People's heritage he bestowed upon her. It was this feeling, this quality of an idyllic interlude shared by two strangers whose lives had finally touched in full sympathy and trust, that held them both: two happy children wandering hand in hand, on an Indian Summer day, in the mountains of old New Mexico . . .

"Good world!" said Inocencio. "Nothin' spoiled. I showin' you!"

There was so much to show and see! Flowers, trees and plants, the birds of the air, the fish of the waters, the animals of the earth. The living stones. The great breathing mountains themselves. All kachina forces of the invisible universe, embodying for a brief time these physical shapes and forms before returning once again to the eternal reservoir. Everything, all at once, came joyously alive with new smells and sounds and shapes Elsie had never known before.

There was the small, crinkly-leaved peppermint one sucked in tall glasses of iced tea and snatched from Mother's mint juleps; the larger, stronger, and smooth-leaved horsemint that Inocencio said Indians dried for tea and cooked with their meat; the healing herb *oshá*; and globules of clear, hard sap which Inocencio picked off from the trunk of a giant spruce and gave the girl to chew. "Chewin' gum! Indian don't have to go to store." At a clump of willows he cut off two short stems. Handing one to Elsie, he chewed the end of the other until it was a soft white brush. "Indian got toothbrush, too!"

Elsie, laughing with pleasure, pointed to a gray squirrel chattering on a branch above them. "Look at his bushy tail! He's just like the one Pilar made for me!"

Farther up the trail Inocencio stopped to show her some tiny hoof marks. "Him deer. He runnin'. Scared!"

"But why, Inocencio?"

Patiently, the old Indian sought and found the answer, the imprint of a soft pad. "Cat. He hungry. That why."

"Just a cat? Why?"

"Mountain cat. Wild cat. Lion. But he no catch him," Inocencio added confidently.

It all seemed so plain to him, as if he were reading it out of a book. But still Elsie persisted. "Why?"

Inocencio looked up at an eagle circling above the cliffs. "Eagle good friend deer. All time he tell him when hunter comin'." It was very strange, this close friendship between the deer and the eagle. But there was also an affinity between the locust and the mountain sheep, the snake and the antelope, and other notable pairs of wild creatures. "Indian know," he said mysteriously. "We do them dances about them things."

The girl was frightened by a gray ghostly shape that flapped up noisily before her and flitted silently into the high dark shadows of the trees until she learned that it was merely a big, blue mountain grouse. A few minutes later she ran out of the brush to pull at Inocencio's blanket. "It's a mean old thing! I went to pat him and he bristled up like Mother's pin cushion!" Inocencio peered out at the little monster. "Ai. Him just porcupine."

The trail rose higher and the canyon widened out to a grove of aspens. Half the trees were chopped off close to the ground. Elsie could see the fine chiseled marks on the V-shaped cuts. Inocencio put a hand over her mouth, and cautiously she followed him through the brush. Wiggling slowly on their bellies, they finally stopped and peered through the thick grass. Before them the stream was blocked by a beaver dam, forming a still, glassy pond. Mosquitoes buzzed about her like little airplanes, but she was careful to make no fuss in brushing them away. In a little while the still surface of the pond was broken by a ripple. It kept moving toward the dam. Then she saw something with a small head, sharp protruding teeth, and a flat tail climb up on the dam.

Excited, she clutched Inocencio's shoulder. Instantly, the animal slapped down his wet, flat tail with a loud report and dived back into the water. "Don't tell me what he is!" the girl shouted. "He's a beaver and that's the house he made!"

In the bright, hot hush of noon they stopped in a little mountain meadow where the whitewater stream slowed into a still trout pool. Elsie stripped off her cowboy suit and boots, and wearing only her little pink panties waded out to splash in the water.

"It's cold but it feels good!" she shouted merrily. "Come on in!"

The gay, laughing little girl with her thin, childish body bore little resemblance to the hard, sophisticated and malicious child Inocencio had first seen. He watched her indulgently. Then stripping off his blanket and shirt, and unbraiding his pigtails, he washed his hair. He was still drying it in the sun when Elsie, sopping wet and shivering, waded up to splash water on him.

"Ai! Ai! It cold!" he grumbled goodnaturedly, picking up his blanket and drying her with gentle hands.

Elsie, dressed again, sat on the bank watching him dry his hair. It spread out on his shoulders long and loose like a woman's, blacker than anything she had ever seen. Not the glossy blue-black of Spanish people's hair, but a lusterless ink-black in which every hair seemed a separate and living strand. Through it he kept running his dark fingers, flipping it up, shaking it loose. As he did so, the girl could see the muscles rippling under his smooth, firm-fleshed arms and shoulders. This was the first time the girl had seen his bare body, stripped to the waist, and it struck her again with its womanly softness. His breasts were not muscularly outlined like a man's, but deep and soft like a woman's. Freddie's

[104]

chest was covered with curly hair; she had seen him shaving in the bathroom with his shirt off once. Inocencio's broad, soft chest didn't have a hair on it. Elsie noticed the color of his skin, too. It wasn't red as a Redskin's was supposed to be; it was a pale copper like iodine, and in the sunlight it shone smooth as gold. The sight of him disturbed her a little. She felt like cuddling up against him. Then suddenly she felt a giggle coming on; he looked so much like a woman sitting there combing out her long, loose hair.

Inocencio ignored her. Taking his time, he shook out his dry hair, parted it neatly into two tresses, and began to braid them into two long pigtails. When he finished one and flipped it carelessly over his shoulder, Elsie's giggle finally erupted.

"Inocencio! You did that just like a woman!" She flopped over on her back and lay laughing.

"*Cómo no?*" said Inocencio calmly. He finished braiding his other pigtail, and put on his shirt and blanket. "Puttin' on paint now. Just like White womans."

He strode off to the hillside where he had noticed an outcrop of reddish clay. Elsie watched him dig out a pinch, knead it in his palm, and then paint the straight part across the top of his head. With the remainder he rouged his high cheek bones.

Elsie was delighted. "It's war paint! I want some too!"

The old Indian gravely rouged her cheeks with the tip of his finger. "Washin' hair and paintin' for dancin' and them kiva doin's. For feelin' good too. Now we take what comin,' good and bad, just like water in the creek."

They ate lunch—two trout, the last piece of dry cheese, and a handful of squaw berries—and strolled slowly back down the canyon. Elsie, hop-skipping along the narrow trail in front of Inocencio, stopped to jerk up by the roots a clump of scarlet flowers which she held out to show him. The old Indian's pleasant face grew stern. "That Indian paint-brush. He won't never grow

[105]

no more. You kill him. No good killin' things for nothin'." He stopped and gently broke off the long stems of some columbines to hand her, and walked on without comment.

They arrived back at camp. It was just like getting home after a long trip, everything looked so dear and familiar. It had been such a wonderful day! Elsie's eyes sparkled with happiness. With the spontaneity of a child she threw her arms around Inocencio and snuggled up close to him. "I like you! I don't care now if we ever go home again!"

Carried away with enthusiasm for this beautiful spot she now knew so intimately, the girl broke away from him and strutted around the glade like a young bride inspecting a building site. "We'll build us a house right here and stay forever! We'll have a nice bathroom just like Mother's with pretty perfume bottles on all the shelves. We'll hang nice curtains on all the windows . . . I want a chaise-longue, too—just like the one Mother had in Paris. Gold brocade, Inocencio! Let's do that, shall we?"

The old Indian, seated on a log, began to sag in his blanket. All day long he had proudly shown her how one could exist in his native wilderness without the material luxuries of White people. The little girl loved it. Yet without realizing it, she was now betraying to him her unconscious longing for the way of her own people. This lust to destroy natural beauty and transform it into something else! It seemed to be born in White people! Inocencio shrugged sadly without answering.

"Well, maybe we can't. We don't even have a hammer and some nails to build us a house," Elsie continued to prattle cheerfully. "But you can come live with us, Inocencio!" She clapped her hands at the prospect. "That'll be fun! You and Mother can give cocktail parties together and get tight all you want and I won't care. And Mary will cook you all the steaks you want. And we'll go to the movies and have fun together . . . Because I like you better than ANYBODY—EVER!"

Inocencio lowered his head to his clasped hands and said gravely, "Can't goin' back now. Policemens mad. Puttin' me in jail sure."

With this sudden admission of the stark reality which the girl had childishly forgotten, their idyllic interlude was over. Elsie's body stiffened. A look of apprehension returned to her eyes. But still she said loyally, "I don't care if we don't go back, Inocencio. They'll never catch us!"

Yet the comforts and luxuries she had recalled still tugged at her senses. "But it would be nice to have something good to eat for a change, wouldn't it? I'm tired of just meat and fish and coffee, aren't you?" she asked wistfully. "Let's have an omelette or a souffle, sometime. Some vichyssoise would taste good, too, if you knew how to make it cold and thick like Mary. And a napoleon! Oh, I haven't had a napoleon since I was in New York!"

A change had come over Inocencio during her innocent and heartbreaking prattling. He seemed to age into an old, ragged Indian fleeing from a murder with a White child he must no longer keep with him. As his slow, simple mind grasped this tardy realization, his dark kind face hardened with the stern resolve of inescapable reality. He rose and took her by the hand.

"Mebbe we go to that town. El Zaguan. Buy somethin' good to eat, no?"

They walked swiftly out of the glade.

El Zaguan was a village as villages were on these remote, high mountain slopes—a sparse straggle of thick-walled adobes along the rutted dirt road that, tiring of its climb, gave up the struggle and crawled out of sight under the thick growth of piñon. All the adobes were red-brown like the earth they rose from, and unlike those in the valleys below had high pitched roofs of rusty tin to shed the winter snows. There was little to distinguish the buildings. Yet one recognized a general store, a bar with a faded sign reading "*Cantina del Tepeyac*," a house whose front parlor served as the post office, and a few dwellings. The tiny church with its wooden bell tower stood at the far end of town. Discreetly back on the mountain slope squatted a massive building without windows, but with a huge cross planted in front of its hand-hewn door—the *Penitente morada*. It all had the flavor of an ancient settlement that electricity and the radio had never reached, and whose sole reading matter was the mail order catalogue.

Inocencio, standing with Elsie at the edge of town, surveyed it carefully in the fading afternoon sun. There were no cars in sight. A single horse dozed head down at the hitching rack in front of the cantina. Across the road a few men, weighed down by the torpor of a prolonged siesta, squatted in front of the general store. A bedraggled rooster and a stray pig wandered along the street—the only sign of life.

The old Indian still hesitated, looking at the village and then at Elsie. His deliberate mind finally reached a decision: to abandon Elsie here where she would be safe, to obtain a few necessary supplies, and then to strike out alone through the mountain pass.

"Nice peoples here," he informed her casually. "Give anybody good bed. Give anybody ride to Santa Fe sometime."

"But we don't want to go back there, Inocencio!" she reminded him tartly.

"No forget what I sayin'." He handed back to Elsie the purse he had been carrying. "You tired walkin'. Buyin' soda pop now. In that cantina."

"Where are you going?" Elsie asked suspiciously.

"Buyin' groceries. That other place."

"Why can't I go with you?"

"No! I say it!" Resolutely he stepped out into the road.

Elsie followed him with a wondering stare. "How are you going to buy groceries without any money, Inocencio?"

The old Indian halted and took the purse she handed him. "Take all the money you want," Elsie offered generously. "There's lots left."

He thumbed through the bills slowly. When one goes on a noonday picnic, one must take many things; there are never enough good things to eat. But when one is fleeing to hide in the mountains alone all winter, he must restrict himself to bare necessities: salt, sugar, coffee, and matches. Inocencio put temptation from him. He took out a single bill and gave Elsie back her purse. "I thankin' you," he said gravely. Pulling his blanket up to his eyes, and ignoring the loafers in front of the store, he walked quickly inside.

Elsie walked timidly across the street and entered the cantina. There was only one customer seated at the bar, a big man in a leather vest whose seams were hand sewn with sinew. Perching on a stool beside him, Elsie watched him finish his drink without looking at her, set down his empty jigger beside a bottle of bourbon, and go out. When he mounted his horse and rode away, Elsie sat looking around the empty cantina.

Except for the mahogany bar, there were no furnishings save a pot-bellied wood-stove, a rough table and a few chairs, one of which had been badly splintered when someone had thrown it, like a concluding argument, at a rival debater. Two prints hung on the walls. The one in back of the bar was of a humble, dark-faced woman clad in a mantle of sky blue dotted with stars like toasted maize grains. She was the ancient *Tonantzin*, Goddess of the Earth and Corn, Mother of the Aztec gods, for whose altar-Hill of Tepeyac the cantina had been named; for four centuries now sanctified as the Dark Madonna of the Tepeyac, *la Virgen Morena*, the *Santísima Guadalupaña*, our Virgin Guadalupe.

The other hung on the wall opposite her. It was a calendar print of a nude woman lying on her side, back turned to display the nobly magnificent proportions of her lush bottom. Also a *morena*, she wore a rose over her ear; and she was peeping over her shoulder at the woman discreetly eyeing her across the room.

The two women had much in common. They both were faded and fly-specked, weary and worn out from helplessly confronting in the other that conflicting and complementary half of the dual nature that makes all women, saints and sinners, kin. Elsie was not sure which attracted her more. She glanced from one to the other, and then toward the partition in back behind which she could hear the bartender. In a moment he came out and ambled up to her, a fat man with a pock-marked face curiously eyeing her as she dug out a dime from her purse.

"I want a coke!" demanded Elsie boldly.

"Coke? *No hay coke . . . Soda para la niña?*"

"Strawberry, please!"

The bartender shrugged; he returned to the back of the cantina and began rummaging around for a bottle of soda.

Elsie waited. She read the label on the whiskey bottle, took out the cork and sniffed it. Nervous and fidgety, she kept twisting around to keep an eye on the store across the street. Inocencio appeared in the doorway. He looked warily up and down the road, then came out and strode quickly into the brush. A look of panic flitted over Elsie's face. She jumped down from her stool, grabbed the whiskey bottle off the bar, and bolted out the door after him.

As she was disappearing into the brush, the bartender ambled back blowing dust off a bottle of stale soda. Only to find the strange Anglo *niña* gone and his bottle of bourbon gone with her. He rushed to the door shouting at the loafers sitting across the street, "*Madre de Dios! A dónde van? La niña y la botella! Ambos, Sénores!*"

The men, finally awakened, leapt to their feet and ran to the side of the road, staring into the brush into which the two strangers had vanished . . .

Clutching the bottle of whiskey, Elsie kept running after Inocencio. Her face was frantic with fear. "Inocencio! . . . Inocencio!" There was no answer. She increased the pace of her frantic pursuit, plunging down a canyon, struggling up the opposite slope. The sun was sinking; long shadows reached out to grab her. The thick chaparral tore her clothes, scratching her face. On top of a ridge she finally caught a glimpse of his blanketed figure striding swiftly through the trees. With a resurgence of strength, she collected her breath and gave a last piercing scream. "Inocencio!"

The old Indian, deep in the trees, halted and turned around with a scowl. As if unable to go forward or to turn back, he stood listening to the rumble of rocks and the crashing in the thicket as the girl plunged down the slope. In a few minutes the child caught up with him, falling at his feet. "You didn't wait for me, Inocencio!" she gasped between sobs. "It wasn't fair . . . Going off without me . . . It wasn't fair!" Lifting her scratched, tear-stained face, she held up the bottle. "And I was bringing you a present, too!"

The old Indian stood looking at her with an inscrutable face. Finally, he stooped and took the whiskey bottle, tipping it up for a greedy swig. His face softened. Without a word, he lifted her to his shoulder. Then grasping the bottle and his paper sack of supplies with one hand, he strode on in the gathering dusk.

The posse had reached the Jenkins Ranch. Its cars were drawn up in the yard between the house and the barn. Inside the kitchen Mrs. Jenkins was watching Honey and Margaret finish a pot of tea.

Both women looked tired and dusty from their slow ride behind the other cars churning through the sage. For Honey there had been the additional strain of sitting all day in the car with Dixon, whom she persistently ignored. But often she found herself staring at the back of his neck as if she had not kissed it on the pillow beside her. She turned her head away to stare out again at the empty, illimitable sea of sage, conjuring the inexhaustible possibilities of what had happened to Elsie, what the child might be doing, saying, thinking at that very moment.

Mrs. Jenkins noisily scratched a match with her thumbnail and lit the lamp on the table. Honey leaned forward in its flare.

"I tell you, he was the one!" she repeated with a stubborn voice.

"He wasn't no Apache, that's for sure," Mrs. Jenkins explained again patiently. "I been livin' here nigh to twenty years and I know them Jicarillas. He didn't have the face of no Apache. He wasn't built like one. He was bigger and chestier, not skinny and bandy-legged like a horse Indian. He didn't wear no hat, and he wore a blanket. But I didn't see your girl with him."

"My baby was here!"

"I only seen that thievin' Pueblo who stole my bread. But don't you worry none, Ma'am. If your girl's still alive . . . "

"There's no *if* about it!" interrupted Margaret. "Elsie hasn't been harmed all this time and she won't be now!"

There sounded outside the loud barking of the Indian Hater's dogs and men's voices. The three women hurried outside to meet the posse walking into the yard with the rancher, Jenkins.

"They were both here, all right!" Evans called out encouragingly. "The dogs picked up their footprints on the edge of the big pasture!"

"What are we waiting for then?" cried Honey to the men. "Who'll go with me to find my baby? Now!"

The men roared acclaim for her beauty and spirit. All during the trip they had admired the get-up-and-go of this indomitable mother who refused to be left behind. And now she did indeed strike the commanding pose of a beautiful woman ready to assume their leadership as she stood, right arm upraised, her hair falling loose on her shoulders. There was something too dramatic, exhibitive, or something else about that pose, thought Margaret. At that moment she happened to glimpse on Dixon's face a look she had never seen, even during Honey's insults. A sudden suspicion jumped into her mind. "Could he be thinking what I'm thinking?" she wondered.

The look on Dixon's face changed to one of concern. "You don't know what you're saying, Honey!" he said sharply. "It's getting dark, and we're all tired and hungry."

"Reckon he's right, Ma'am," said Shorty. "We lost their trail. They's no use tryin' to foller 'em in the dark."

"Could be they stole a horse," added Jenkins. "I can't spot that little white mare in the bunch. If that Pueblo's got a good eye for a horse, he took her all right."

The ranchwoman put her arm around Honey. "You're goin' to stay right here. I'll stir up a good hot supper, and make some comfy beds in the parlor. Ain't that so, Joe?"

Her husband nodded. "We can feed you all and sleep the boys in the barn if you've a mind to."

Shorty spoke up decisively. "We'll do that. We got to have horses in the mornin', too." He looked at Evans. "You and a couple of boys can drive the cars with the wimmen folks up to El Zaguan and wait there for word from us." He turned toward the posse. "All right now, boys. Pick yer lay-downs in the barn."

After a hearty supper in the crowded kitchen all went to bed: the deputies in the barn, the Evans couple, Honey, and Dixon on makeshift beds in the parlor. Honey had been given the pull-down sofa bed, Margaret a canvas cot, and the two men blankets on the hard floor. For an hour they listened to the two Jenkinses doing the stack of dishes. Then the lamp was blown out.

But still another hour later, they could not get to sleep. Every few minutes they could hear Honey rolling and groaning across the room. "Oh, my lost baby! Where is she now, I wonder? So close and yet so far away!" And then again in the darkness, ages later, sounded her plaintive moan. "I only pray she's safe."

Toward midnight another voice suddenly erupted from the darkness. It was Margaret's. "For God's sake shut up, and let us get to sleep! I'm sick of your constant caterwauling. Do you have to remind us every minute what we're here for? Or do you have no regard for anyone's feelings but your own? Whatever the reason for your darling child's escapade, she's a spoiled brat. You blamed it on your husband Richard, and now you're blaming it on Freddie. Why not look at yourself for a change? You've taken Tom away from his office, and me from my own children. Freddie's on no picnic either. Now cut out the dramatics!"

Evans and Dixon on their hard pallets remained silent. Nor did Honey utter a word. In silence they all, at last, fell asleep.

It was not yet midnight when the moon cleared the tops of the pines standing sentinel over Inocencio and Elsie's camp. The old Indian was still squatting on the ground in front of the fading red glow of the fire. He took a swig from the bottle Elsie had brought him, then leaned forward to peer at the little girl on her bed of fir tips. Hungry, worn out and nervous, she was not sleeping well. She moaned softly, rolled over again. The old Indian settled back on his haunches, took another drink.

In a little while Elsie quieted down. Inocencio did not stir. He was in no hurry: there was always time for important and pleasant matters. This was both. He felt good sitting here by a fire at the girl's feet, and there were still a couple of swallows left in the bottle to make him feel better. Inocencio was not in the habit of anticipating the future; he had learned to take things as they came, like water in the creek. Still the night wind had an edge to it, reminding him that Indian Summer would soon be over and that the first frost and snow were not far behind. When would he have all this again—the indulgent night, the peace and companionship, the warmth in his belly? So he savored it slowly. Finishing the bottle, he leaned forward again.

Elsie was breathing steadily; the fingers of her hand had uncurled. Inocencio got quietly to his feet. Stealthily, he rolled up in his blanket the pitifully few remaining supplies and slung it over his shoulder. He picked up his rifle. For a moment he stood looking down at the sleeping girl. No regret nor reluctance showed on his dark face. She would awake in the morning, seek him in the village he had showed her, and be taken back to her people in Santa Fe. By then he would be through the pass, and safely lost to pursuit in the mountains. Resolutely he slipped away into the darkness . . .

Far down the draw a coyote yapped. An owl hooted in the pines. Elsie moaned restlessly, turned over. "Inocencio!" she whimpered sleepily. There was no answer. She sat up, flung back the blanket, and scrambled to her feet.

He was gone. His rifle was gone, the few supplies—everything that had made the place a home. Betrayed, abandoned and alone, she stared wildly around her at the black bristling forest. All its charm and security had vanished. There was only the menacing moan of the wind in the pine tips, the suspicious splashing of the stream. She herself had changed. She was no longer the pampered, spoiled child who had willfully paraded her selfishness through the cafes and resort hotels of New York, Lisbon, Paris and London. She was simply a small child in torn clothes and with a scratched face who found herself abandoned in the middle of night in the fearsome depths of a mountain wilderness.

Again sounded the soft, eerie hoot of the owl. Petrified by fear, her teeth clamped on her little knotted fist, Elsie stood staring into the forest. The owl dropped from its branch and flitted noiselessly across the glade, a gray ghostly shape in the moonlight. Elsie, head

[115]

upflung and hands clenched, let out a piercing scream . . . another . . . and still another . . .

Inocencio, climbing swiftly up the canyon, turned to catch the sound on the wind. High-pitched and tenuous, it had the frightened-child texture of the scream of a cougar. When it came again, more short of breath and hysterical, he knew what it was. A feeling of cold dismay clutched and held him. Nothing was harming the girl. There was no need for her to be scared. She needed only to throw a stick on the fire and wait until morning to walk into the village. He could not be saddled in his flight by a small White girl, and this was his last chance to get free of her.

Still the old Indian hesitated in darkness and silence. Crazy little White girl! What if she was so frightened she ran into the forest and hurt herself in the dark? Inocencio had never had trouble making up his mind; the indecision was torturing. He knew now, beyond all foolish hopes, what it would mean if he went back. Yet during these six mad days something had touched the quick of his being that he had never felt before. What it was he did not know, but it had the shape of a child's trust and her arms around him. Another last terrified scream from below confirmed it. He turned around and plunged back down the steep trail.

Elsie, hearing the crashing of his body through the thicket, froze in a posture of abject fear from which she was suddenly released by his appearance on the edge of the clearing. She hurtled forward, threw herself at him, and clutched him around the legs.

"Inocencio! It's you and I thought you were a bear!" Her small body, shaken with sobs, cowered against him. "You were running away from me! Inocencio! Don't leave me to the bears! Don't leave me!"

The old Indian set down his blanket roll and his rifle. Slowly his long arms reached out and wrapped around her. In a deep, tender and compassionate voice he gave himself up to his fate.

"I not leavin' you, cowboy. No more. I say it."

[116]

Day broke clear and clean—the seventh and last day of their strange and wonderful, terrible and tragic flight. Long, long ago in timeless time, on an Indian Summer day during Fiesta in Santa Fe, the mysterious power that charts the flight of swallows across the sea and draws a moth to the flame had marked their own course. There was no turning back.

By sunup they were in the pass—the narrowing, steep-walled *zaguan* passing under the lee of the high, sheer cliffs they had glimpsed far out on the desert. The lower end of the valley was still wide enough to be intercut with low ridges of coarse brown tufa, once an immense lava flow erupted from the volcanic peak above. Between them were narrow side-canyons choked with brush, tall stands of pine and patches of knee-high grass watered by hidden springs seeping up through the porous rock. In this tangled maze Inocencio found the ancient trail winding up and across the ridge. It was a narrow groove worn ankle deep or more into the soft rock by uncounted generations of naked feet. The old Indian's moccasins, one placed in front of the other at each step, fitted into it naturally and without effort as he strode in the lead. Elsie, struggling behind in her boots, straddled it or jumped across it from side to side.

"Where are we going now?" she kept asking plaintively.

"We goin'. You see," Inocencio answered cryptically.

They kept climbing up the steadily rising trail. At the base of the cliff wall, near the top of the ridge, the trail ended abruptly in a series of hand-and-toe holes cut into a steep defile through the huge rock fragments of the talus slope. It was a natural defensive gateway just wide enough for a climber to squeeze through; a man standing above it with a stone axe, centuries ago, could have held an enemy tribe at bay. Inocencio, pausing for breath, appraised it with approval before beginning to climb through it.

Elsie loitered behind, staring at the petroglyphs which covered the face of the cliff. Some of the carvings reminded her of the mural figures painted on the wall of the kiva in the deserted city where they had spent the night. There was the same plumed serpent crawling across the rock, the man with corn stalks sticking up from his head, a curious maze, and a sunwheel. The animals and birds she recognized at once. A deer with horns. A wonderful bear with a big eye and open mouth, and down near a crack in the wall the imprint of his foot, just like a man's hand. She liked the turkey and the little birds, too, but the masked faces and the queer humpbacked flute player were strange to her. All the carvings looked like figures scrawled by a child on a blackboard. Yet like all things Indian, they had a dimensional quality foreign to her. Both attracted and repelled by them, she suddenly and carelessly slipped on the loose gravel and with a frightened scream rolled down the talus slope.

Inocencio, hearing her cry, whirled around and plunged down after her. When he reached her, Elsie was sitting up, grasping one foot and crying with pain. She was a pathetic sight: her cowboy suit was torn and dusty, her face was scratched afresh and bleeding through the dirt.

"It's this one I hurt, Inocencio," she whimpered. "This one here."

Inocencio knelt and took off her boot. She had twisted her ankle and the flesh was beginning to swell. The old Indian's face darkened. He looked down at her and then up at the pass. It was no use. They had reached the end of their flight.

Gently, but with a somber face, he picked her up and began his laborious climb back up the slope.

"Where are we going? What are we going to do now, Inocencio?"

The old Indian did not answer; he was breathing hoarsely, and a thin trickle of sweat was running down his big nose. Step by step he struggled up the steep slope of the ridge to the base of the pinkish-white cliffs that formed its upper rampart. Here, unnoticeable from far below, extended hundreds of tiny caves hollowed out of the rocky wall. They were everywhere: squeezed into vertical faults, dug under great overhanging ledges, pecked into the butter-smooth pinkish rock itself by the stone axes of their prehistoric occupants. Inocencio found a nice one overlooking the valley below, and set Elsie down.

"We here," he panted, stretching out to rest.

These two simple words told for him the whole story of their tragic flight, and indeed of his whole life. For Inocencio, unable to conform to his pueblo's life and to adjust to the impinging White world, had sought to escape it in drunkenness. Confronted at last by a murder he had committed, and by forces he had set in motion which he did not understand, he had been compulsively driven back into his own racial past. The whole course of his flight with Elsie had attested to it: back into Indian country, back to the first great ground-pueblo of his people, back to his own root-mountains, and finally back to these primitive cliff-dwellings where his earliest prehistoric ancestors took shelter long before they developed the tribal organization and architectural skills to build a communal pueblo. Now he could go no further. His regression was complete. He had reached not only the end of his flight, but his last oubliette . . . And he knew it deep down inside him; like an animal, he knew it. It was reflected in his somber face, his wary manner, his heavy silence.

But he was also a man, an old man who had duties to perform. He brought water from a spring below, built a fire, and bathed Elsie's swollen foot. Then he wrapped it with herbs in a piece torn off from his blanket. Of their supplies there was now left only salt, sugar and coffee. He took his rifle and went out again. How familiar it all seemed: a small clan group . . . a single family . . . a man and a woman making a home in a tiny cave, trudging down the

[119]

steep trail for water from the spring, hunting food in the wilderness, watching warily from the cliff-top for signs of approaching enemies. It was the prototypal pattern of his people's earliest existence. Inocencio gave himself to it fully; somehow it seemed complete.

While he was gone, Elsie examined the cave with childish interest. The floor was a thick layer of fine dust. Sifting it through her fingers, she brought up a few shards of broken pottery. One of them was quite pretty after she spit on it and rubbed it clean; the color was a deep red, with black markings. Poking around some more she unearthed a corn cob and then a stick of charcoal which she threw aside. Some picnickers had been here a long time ago and built a fire in the corner. The roof was still blackened by its smoke where flakes of rock had not peeled off. Who they were and where they came from she did not know or care. Yet Christ had not yet trudged to Calvary when they first wandered over the land seeking water and shelter from storms and enemies, following game, and bringing with them the miracle and mystery of Indian maize—America's corn. A new people on a new and unknown continent, a rude primitive people dressed in the skins of animals they killed and in robes of turkey feathers. Weaving watertight baskets to cook in, then learning to make pottery. Planting the roots of a civilization. Generation after generation, century upon century, filing down the steep slope to their tiny corn patches, carrying up water jars on their heads, their bare feet wearing the trail ever deeper into the bare rock.

It was a nice cave, just big enough for two! Elsie began to play house. She smoothed out the fine dust, spread a blanket to sit on. She arranged their few belongings neatly against the back wall. She poked back into the fire the popping cedar sparks. Then she sat looking out the mouth of the cave at the world below. It was just like the big picture window in her mother's apartment in

Paris. She could see everything: the narrow little valley choked with brush, pine and piñon, flanked on the opposite side by the low ridge behind which lay the village of El Zaguan.

In a little while Inocencio came back with a cottontail he had skinned and cleaned. She watched him cut it up and put it on the fire to roast.

"Now. That good," he said cheerfully.

While it was cooking, Elsie clambered painfully to the top of the cliff. The view here was even better. She could see over the ridge to the far-off village. She sat down to watch. At first El Zaguan was empty and still of life: a toy village of little cardboard houses mounted on a board, like a Christmas present she once had received from Germany. Then suddenly it came alive.

She waited a bit, then called out excitedly, "I can see the town, Inocencio! You ought to look. There's lots of cars coming in. Lots of 'em! And look at the people. They must be going to have a fiesta!"

Inocencio bounded out of the cave and climbed up to join her. Small but distinguishable in the distance, automobiles were rolling into the single street of the village—a station wagon, a big touring sedan, a black car with letters on the side, several more cars. People from the store, cantina and houses were running out to talk with the strangers getting out of the cars.

Inocencio jerked Elsie to her feet. "They comin'," he said quietly but tensely.

"Who, Inocencio?"

Without answering, he took her back down into the cave. Quickly stamping out the fire, he covered it with dirt so there would be no smoke. The rabbit was not fully done, but he cut off a piece for each of them and sprinkled it with salt. Elsie took a bite and complained, "But it isn't cooked, Inocencio. I don't like it. And we don't have any bread or anything to go with it."

[121]

"You eatin' just the same," he answered curtly. "Mebbe long time we don't get nothin' more." He chewed up his own piece rapidly.

Again the girl complained. "You put too much salt on mine. It made me thirsty."

Obediently the old Indian clambered down the slope after water. He loaded his rifle with shells. "They comin'. Them policemens," he said sternly. "You stayin' here. Keepin' quiet." Then he climbed back to the top of the cliffs to keep vigil.

Not since that terrible Good Friday when the local *Cristo* had died on the big cross in the ravine behind the *Penitente morada* just after the *Procesión de Sangre* had there been so much excitement in El Zaguan. The single street of the village swarmed with *máquinas* and strangers, with shopkeepers and women pouring out from their doorways, and with farmers running in from their fields to talk with members of the posse.

To Honey, sitting in Evans' limousine, the excitement reflected to some degree her own inner tension. The dragging worry about Elsie's safety had been lifted at Jenkins' Ranch with the discovery she was alive and well. But it had been replaced by an insatiable desire to catch up with her and her Indian kidnapper. This internal pressure had not been alleviated by the unbearable supper. A kitchen crowded with rough, dirty men. Stringy steak and fried potatoes swimming in grease. The flask of cognac she had brought was empty. Pushing her plate aside, she had swallowed some vitamin pills from the bottle she always carried. The night was worse. The hard springs of the sofa biting through the cheap, cotton blanket. The breathing presence of her three companions in the same small room. And then, erupting from the stuffy darkness, Margaret's violent, accusative outburst. Margaret, who always had been so sweet and reassuring! What did it mean? Whatever it meant, if it meant anything more than indigestion from

[122]

those greasy fried potatoes and steak, it kept her uneasily awake until she glimpsed the light of a lantern bobbing past the window and heard roosters crowing. She swallowed the last of her vitamin pills with a cup of bitter, boiled coffee, and left with the cavalcade of cars before sunup. Evans drove his own car, grumbling at the rutted dirt road, and a member of the posse drove each of the other cars. Shorty with the other deputies rode off on horseback, following the Indian Hater and his pack of dogs.

Evans and the first of the cars had reached El Zaguan early, despite the rough and unmarked road. One of the drivers who spoke Spanish picked up the information that both the Indian and the small girl had been in the village. Immediately, he drove back to guide the rest of the posse. While awaiting them, the Evans car remained parked in the street, moving sporadically into shade as the sun kept climbing. How unbearable it was! The four of them sitting there motionless with nothing to say. And the curious villagers ambling up to gawk at them as at strange animals in a cage. None of the Evans party could speak Spanish; they could only stare back in silence.

"What are we waiting for?" shouted Honey. "For God's sake, let's DO something!"

"What?" asked Margaret in a voice curt and ironic. Honey could not think of a reply. They kept waiting.

Eventually all the rest of the posse arrived. Getting out of the car with her companions, Honey watched them milling with the crowd of villagers in hopeless confusion. The bartender from the *Cantina del Tepeyac* was explaining to one group of deputies how Elsie had stolen a bottle of whiskey. To another group the storekeeper was describing Inocencio. Evans, one arm around Margaret, was questioning Shorty. On the side of the road the Indian Hater was unloading and leashing his dogs. And wandering from group to group was Dixon, his baggy flannel trousers showing that they had been slept in.

[123]

In the midst of this confusion a state police car drove up, the two officers demanding to see Shorty. The three men drew off to one side. Honey could not hear their voices, but their gestures were articulate enough. Everybody was angry, everybody was confused. All this needless talk and delay was so exasperating that it made her faint with anger, sick with frustration.

She was aroused by the appearance of the parish priest walking down the street from his church at the far end of town. Honey had never appealed to religion for solace—it was a power too mysterious and complicated for her to attempt to understand, although of course she and Richard had been on excellent social terms with the bishop. Yet the sight of this bareheaded and stalwart man of faith in his long black robe instantly brought to surface Margaret's accusations of her guilty neglect of Elsie and suggested a humble and penitent supplication of divine power to ensure her baby's safety. Everything about him set him apart as an island of divine refuge in a sea of mortal confusion: the anonymity cast over him by his rusty black garb, his sedate walk and grave demeanor, the dead white pallor of his face. Impulsively, she ran to meet him.

As she reached him, she could not help noticing a spot of cooking grease on his robe; she was revolted by his old-fashioned, square-toed, black shoes covered with dust; and she instinctively knew that the splotched pallor of his face was the unhealthy sign of a poor liver. Yet something in his expression and demeanor denied at once these transient manifestations of mortal frailty and confirmed her first impression of him.

"Father! It's my baby! She . . . "

The priest stopped and looked at her solemnly. "*Sí, Señora*. Yes I have been told."

Honey ignored his deplorable accent. "Please make my baby safe when we find her!" she beseeched him, her hand nervously plucking at his sleeve. "I've neglected her and it's all my fault! I couldn't bear it if anything has happened to her. But I'll make it all up if I just get her back safe. I swear to God I will, Father! Please!" Fumbling in her purse she slipped a bill into his hand as if concluding a satisfactory bargain.

The parish priest stuffed it into a pocket of his pants beneath his robe. "God's will be done whatever happens, *Señora*. But I will pray for your child's safety."

At that moment there began a full-throated baying from the dogs. Honey flung around. The Indian Hater, his pack on leash, was drawing off to the side of the road.

Shorty leapt toward him with a profane yell. "Hold on there! God blast yer stinkin' hide! Who told you to start off?"

He had reached the limit of his patience with the Indian Hater. Ever since they had started, the intuitive guesses of the detestable old man had proved right. This was enough to irk him. But it was the condescending aplomb with which the Indian Hater delivered them, always accompanied by a contemptuous squirt of tobacco juice from between his scraggly yellow teeth, that worked on Shorty's nerves. Worse than this was the old man's headstrong nature and indomitable will to have his own way, hell or high water.

Shorty had punched cows too long not to know that a single unruly maverick could stampede a whole herd. This was exactly what the Indian Hater was on the point of doing. He had continually ignored Shorty's authority in front of the whole posse. Now the men were tired, grumpy and restless after three days on the trail. They had almost run down their quarry and were keyed up with excitement. Let them get out of hand and anything might happen. Goaded by the old man's monomaniacal hatred for Indians, they might mob the old Indian and harm the little girl with him.

"Damn you!" he yelled. "This is a posse, and it's high time I showed you who's bossin' it!"

There was no doubt in his mind, as he leapt forward, that he was now going to give the old man the beating he deserved. There was no doubt in the Indian Hater's mind either. He whirled around to face Shorty, trying to raise his rifle as a club or at least free the rawhide whip hanging on his wrist. As he did so, the pack of pulling dogs entangled him in their leashes. He went down in a heap, cursing profanely, trying to free himself from a snarled web of leather lines. Shorty jerked the rawhide whip from him, and raising it over his head, waited to step in.

There was a sudden change in attitude among the crowd of men who had rushed up behind him. They saw that Shorty had taken the Indian Hater in hand at last and meant business. One of them grabbed his upraised arm.

"Aw, let him alone, Shorty," he said apologetically. "He ain't so young as he can stand a rawhidin'."

Shorty flung the whip at the Indian Hater who, freed now of the entangling leashes, jumped up and began thrashing his pack of dogs.

"And you, Smith!" demanded the man. "Let them dogs be! We got a need for 'em . . . I say let's go! What we waitin' for?"

"O.K." said Shorty. "Remember, no shootin' less I say so! We're aimin' to take this Indian back to a court trial and without hurtin' the kid! Savvy?"

He led the way into the thick brush. At his shoulder was the Indian Hater, his rifle swinging in the crook of his left arm and his dogs held in leash with his right hand. Behind them the others were falling into line: the armed deputies, two uniformed state police officers, and a motley crowd of villagers carrying guns, clubs, and pitchforks.

Back in the road Evans laid a restraining hand on Honey's arm. "Mrs. Wilbur, it's impossible for you to walk miles through the brush, and I assure you that you'll be in the way. You've given us enough trouble already."

They were interrupted by the bartender whose quick eye had

caught a glimpse of the bill passed to the priest. He came up to them wringing his hands and whining. "*Madre de Dios!* They ask questions. They talk. But nobody pay me for that good whiskey. Four peso's worth it was, and . . . "

Honey gave him a withering look of cold contempt. "My daughter and I always pay our debts to tradesmen." She turned to Evans. "Give him his four dollars, Mr. Evans."

As Evans reached for his wallet, Honey broke free. She ran frantically across the road, and lifting her skirts to clear the brush, vanished after the posse.

Evans, Margaret and Dixon, with despairing looks at each other, followed her.

The sun had climbed to its zenith. The hot hush of an Indian Summer noon fell over the still valley. Nothing moved save a hawk slowly wheeling high overhead.

This was the calm before the storm; and huddling in their tiny cave, the old Indian and the little girl were waiting for it to blow past. The heat and the silence were oppressive.

"They'll never find us here!" boasted Elsie.

"We hidin'," Inocencio agreed calmly. There was indeed little chance that their pursuers would ever find them in this one of hundreds of small caves hidden in a maze of brush-grown canyons. Still he was uneasy, and kept a wary watch on the little valley below.

The girl stared at his dark, impassive face a long time, then shyly moved closer. "You've been good to me, Inocencio. You didn't leave me like my papa did, and you weren't mean to me like Freddie."

Impulsively she flung her arms around him and kissed him on the cheek.

Inocencio did not stir.

"I've kissed you, but you've never kissed me! Not once!" she pouted, drawing back slightly.

"White peoples always kissin' and huggin' like in them movin' pictures! Don't mean nothin'!" He furtively wiped his wet cheek. "Indian don't do them things all a time, but he lovin' just the same."

A little embarrassed by her close, snuggling body, he threw back his blanket and took off his belt with its big buckle of sand-cast silver mounted with a single chunk turquoise—the only thing of value he possessed. "You keep him. Cowboy need belt." He tossed it carelessly into her lap.

Elsie, with a squeal of delight, jumped up to unfasten her own cheap souvenir belt. "You knew mine was worn out! Look! It's just imitation. Paper!" She proudly wrapped Inocencio's belt around her, and fastened to it her toy pistol holster. "Oh, this is a pretty one!" she cried, not minding that it ludicrously hung down almost to her thigh.

"Mebbe get big belly sometime. Then it fit," ventured Inocencio.

"No, I won't. I'll have steam baths and massages and beauty treatments just like Mother. I'll be pretty when I grow up, and I'll have money to spend, too!" She sat down again. "My father gave some to the lawyer to give me when I'm big. That's why you can come and live with us just as soon as these policemen go away when they can't find us!"

The old Indian was beyond indulging in such idle fancies now. He shook his head sadly. "I no goin' anywhere, cowboy. Policemens chasin' me every place. They no forget, them policemens!"

Elsie snuggled up to him with a little shiver of apprehension. "But what are you going to DO, Inocencio?"

His dark, smooth face with its hairless eyebrows did not change expression as he stared impassively out of the mouth of the cave. "Mebbe I die, cowboy. Animals they know when time comin'. Birds too. I feel him here same way." His wrinkled chocolate-brown hand fell lightly on his breast.

"Die! Inocencio! No!"

"Stayin' in jail no good for old Indian. Can't see Our Father Sun when he come up standin'. Can't see the Night People in the sky. No fresh air to breathe. Nothin' good to drink. Not even a little bottle when I feelin' sad. Better dyin'. I say it." There was no fear, no regret in his voice. Just a calm acceptance of the inevitable.

The little girl was frightened. She flung herself against him, held him tight. "I won't let you, Inocencio! I won't! Besides, they won't find us here. Ever!"

The old Indian turned his head to stare down into the empty, silent canyon. "We watchin'," he said calmly.

Suddenly he flung the girl aside, leaning forward on his knees in a posture of alert attention. A moment later Elsie heard it too—the faint but ominous sound of baying hounds.

Inocencio leapt to his feet and threw off his blanket. "Dogs! They usin' dogs to smell us! Now they comin' sure!"

No doubt was left in either of them now. There was no use hiding. The storm would not blow past. It must be met.

They scurried out of the cave, Inocencio climbing swiftly up the steep slope, Elsie limping behind. The old Indian stopped, looking back at the narrow trail along the base of the cliffs. It was too late now to take a stand at the narrow passageway. Yet he discerned another, easier and more obvious means of access—up the steep talus slope itself directly below them. This too was provided with a means of defense. Just above him was a fault in the cliff-wall, a long vertical crevice choked with boulders and loose stones prevented from rolling down only by the roots of a stunted juniper. Immediately, he set to work rolling and lifting more large rocks to set on top.

[129]

"What are you doing that for, Inocencio?" asked the little girl.

He paused to wipe the sweat from his face, pointing down to the bottom of the fault terminating directly above the indistinct trail winding up the steep slope from the floor of the canyon.

"These rocks. I push him down when policemens come. Nobody get us!"

The simple use of an avalanche to crush approaching enemies was as obvious to Elsie now as it had been to the ancient cliff-dwellers. She set to work to help him. She looked ridiculous: hobbling about on her bandaged foot, the huge belt looped around her thin waist and hanging down to her skinny little thigh, and carrying stones that were mere pebbles compared to the huge rocks that Inocencio was heaving into place. Yet her puny efforts bespoke, as nothing else could, the tragic intensity and desperate resolve of this old Indian and small girl to resist the large crowd of armed men approaching.

Both stopped as the silence was broken by the deep-throated baying of the hounds entering the canyon. They stared anxiously into the peaceful little valley below, not yet disturbed by any visible life. Inocencio grabbed Elsie by the arm.

"You gettin' in cave! Quick, cowboy! Not comin' out, no matter what!"

They stared at each other for a long moment. The time had come. Each knew it.

A change came over Elsie. She was no longer the sweet, cuddlesome child of a few minutes ago, but the hard and aggressive girl Inocencio had first seen—a girl with the world against her, a woman ready to fight with her man to defend their wilderness home. She yanked out a dirty red bandana from her pants and looped it around her neck.

"Tie it in back for me, Inocencio," she said harshly. "I want to be a real cowboy. A bad one!"

When he had knotted it in back, she slipped the handkerchief up over her face to her eyes like a mask. Then she took out her toy pistol from its tiny holster.

"We'll kill 'em, Inocencio. Kill 'em all!"

She scurried down into the cave. Inocencio picked up his rifle, slipped a shell into the breech, and stepped behind a boulder.

He did not have long to wait. There burst into sight in the canyon below the baying hounds held in leash by the gaunt, buckskin-jacketed Indian Hater, followed by Shorty and several deputies—the vanguard of the large posse. Inocencio raised his rifle and fired.

At the sound of its sudden sharp crack, the men stopped at the mouth of the canyon. The Indian Hater instinctively drew up his rifle. Shorty at his shoulder knocked it down.

"Hell! That old galoot ain't goin' to give us no trouble! It's only a twenty-two!"

He felt immensely relieved, as if the whole weight of the chase had been lifted from him. The old Indian had let them know where he was by his careless and premature shot. There was no need to track him to his hiding place, no fear of being shot from ambush. Still, he prudently pulled the Indian Hater out of the sunlight into the shade of the brush until the rest of the posse caught up with them.

The shot, however, had thrown the straggling crowd behind him into a pandemonium. The vanguard of deputies was scattering in all directions, dodging behind rocks and trees from which they cautiously peered out to determine where the shot came from and to catch a glimpse of their quarry.

"We've run him down!"

"Watch yourselves, boys! He means business!"

Their loud shouts and the echo of the shot, thrown back and forth from the sides of the canyon, stirred more alarm in the stragglers to the rear. Men nervously snapped off the safety locks

[131]

of their rifles or hoisted their pitchforks higher, and hurried through the chaparral. Evans and Dixon stopped in dismay. It was evident that Margaret between them could go no faster; pale and gasping, she looked played out.

"They've found them!" Evans panted. "We've got to go on and find Mrs. Wilbur before she does something crazy. Just follow the broken brush. You'll have no trouble. And don't worry!" The two men rushed on.

Honey, ahead of them, heard Evans' anxious call, "Mrs. Wilbur! Where are you?" And then Dixon's shrill cry. "Honey! For God's sake! Wait!"

Ignoring them, she caught her breath and plunged on through the thick brush, passing one group of men after another. At the mouth of the canyon she broke out into the clear and stood panting. Her dress was torn. Bloody scratches showed through the rents in her sheer nylons. A twig still stuck in her disheveled hair. With wild staring eyes, she flung herself at Shorty.

"You've found her! Where is she?" she screamed.

Shorty whirled around and shoved her behind a boulder. "Mrs. Wilbur! You ain't got no call to be here, Ma'am!"

"I want my child!"

"We'll git her without no heesterics," he said curtly.

The little valley was quiet now. The men crept forward, gathering about Shorty. In the silence he stepped forward, looked up at the cliffs, and cupped his hands.

"I-No-Cen-Cio! . . . Hey! You up there . . . Come on down peaceful fore we come git you!"

Another shot sounded from high above—the sharp ping of a small-bore rifle and the faint whine of its spent lead. Shorty grinned and stepped back.

"That's what I wanted! On'y to see jest where he was anyway. That pea-shooter won't do no harm less'n we rush him, which we ain't!"

He turned to the two uniformed state policemen. "Why don't you be obligin' and hike around the end of the ridge, so's he can't give us the slip? I don't figure he'll go over the ridge, but you can make sure he don't."

As they moved off, he called to one of his deputies. "Jackson, you and some other boys climb up that old trail to the left of him. Don't crowd him. Jest let him see you . . . No shootin', mind! We don't know where the girl is yet!"

Then he stepped behind the boulder to confront Honey. "Now, Ma'am. I can leave a man right here to make sure you don't bother nobody. Or you can come with us and behave yourself without no fuss. Heads or tails, Ma'am?"

"Don't make me stay here!" begged Honey.

Shorty took her by the arm and keeping back in the brush, led the group toward the base of the steep slope. He felt easy, confident that he had everything under control. "Yes sir!" he said half-jokingly to the Indian Hater beside him. "You're stayin' right here where I can keep an eye on you!"

To Inocencio the sight of the men gathering below was far less reassuring. The dogs had picked up his scent again and were straining at their leashes in full cry. The men still waited in the shadows of the cottonwoods; but there was no telling when, like foolish White men, they might storm up the slope.

He was more disturbed by a movement far down in the lower end of the valley. The two state police officers were breaking cover and going around the ridge. The sheen of their blue uniforms and the glitter of their polished buttons struck the old Indian with all the force of impersonal and implacable authority. He flung a helpless glance upward at the smooth and unscalable cliff wall above him.

He was alarmed now by the sudden sight of still more men

[133]

climbing the narrow, ancient trail to his right. Once they gained access to the caves, into which they could dodge in and out, they could advance upon him with full protection. Confronted by the men below him, and his escape to the rear blocked, Inocencio was stung to action by the approach of this third group along the trail. Crouching behind his boulder, he fired shot after shot to hold them back.

The men ducked for cover and scurried into caves, but kept slowly advancing. Ignoring Shorty's orders, they began to fire back. The canyon began to throb with the loud roars of their big-bore rifles, punctuated by the sharp, thin cracks from Inocencio's twenty-two.

Elsie in her cave could see and hear it all: men along the trail to her right dodging behind rocks to fire their big guns; Inocencio, hidden behind his big boulder to her left, popping his twenty-two; the bullets kicking up little spurts of dust on the slope; the shouting men below; the baying of the excited dogs; the roars of the guns echoing throughout the canyon. The fight had begun! A real fight! Roused to a frenzy of excitement, she crouched melo-dramatically, whipping out her toy pistol and firing at them all.

"Bang! Bang! Fall dead!" she shouted with childish rage.

It was this quality that made her such a precocious, problem child—the ability to give in, completely and instantly, to her tre-mendous imagination. She flung herself belly down on the floor of the cave, legs spread out and pistol propped up, squinting for better aim over her bandana mask.

Far below her, Honey crouched behind a rock, gnawing her clenched fist in an effort to restrain her anguished worry. It was little matter to her that Evans, worried about his wife, slipped away to seek her back down the canyon. Nor did she pay any attention to Dixon squatting stubbornly beside her. All her thoughts were preternaturally centered on that small, childish body she had not yet glimpsed, whose presence she felt but whose whereabouts still remained uncertain, and whose safety was endangered by the firing all around her.

"Don't shoot! You'll hit my girl!" she screamed wildly. "Damn you! Please!"

No one heard her above the racket of the dogs which the Indian Hater was lashing and kicking in a frantic effort to tie them to a tree. Nor could anyone hear Shorty angrily shouting as he waved back the men who were disobeying his orders.

"Cut it out! I told you no shootin'! Git back!"

As a last attempt he threw down his rifle and stepped out into the open in full view of the pursued and pursuers, raising his empty hands over his head. The firing dwindled away into silence. He shouted up at the cliffs again.

"You! Inocencio! . . . We got you cornered! Step out and put yer hands up!"

For a moment there was no sound nor movement on the slope above. Inocencio was frantically opening the breech of his rifle, searching the pockets of his pants. He had run out of shells. The old Indian threw down his rifle in disgust. Then drawing himself up in a posture of proud defiance, he stepped from behind the boulder and let out a yell of derision.

"Hi-yah! . . . Ai! . . . Hi-yah!"

The eerie war whoop, shrill as the scream of a hawk and pitched off key, rose high and straight as a feathered lance, shook in the thin breeze, and shattered against the walls of the cliffs, its echoes sounding and resounding in the silence. It was a sound which this mountain canyon had echoed for centuries on end, but which it would never echo again.

Elsie stiffened with fear in her cave, little cold shivers chasing up her back . . . Honey shuddered behind her boulder below, covering her face and ears with both hands . . . The Indian Hater's thin lips drew back from his tobacco-stained teeth in a snarl as he reached for his rifle.

[135]

Only Shorty remained calm and self-possessed. Boldly walking to the base of the steep slope, he shouted up again.

"Send the girl down, Inocencio! Then you come down peaceful! We won't hurt you none! I promise!"

The old Indian hesitated. He had one more chance now. He could send Elsie down; and while she was slowly picking her way down the slope on her bandaged foot, he could make a last desperate run. He glanced longingly up at the narrowing pass, then down toward the cave.

Elsie, as if reading his mind, suddenly burst out of the cave, clambering toward him. "Don't let them get me! Inocencio! Don't leave me! You promised!"

The first sight of her child after an agonizing week of doubt and despair was too much for Honey. She leapt out from behind her shelter and ran across the clearing with a piercing scream. "Elsie! My baby! Elsie!"

Behind her the crowd of deputies burst forth, running toward the foot of the trail ascending the slope.

All of this at once, in a simultaneity of sound and motion, goaded Inocencio into a last desperate act. "I not leavin' you, cowboy! They don't get us!" He leapt to the top of the crevice stacked with rocks. Fully exposed, he braced legs and arms against the big boulder to start the avalanche crashing down upon the running crowd.

"Mother! . . . It's my mommy! . . . Mother!"

The thin, childish scream arrested Inocencio. Braced for a powerful shove, he twisted his face sideways for a quick glimpse at Elsie. She had stopped halfway across the slope, and was staring down unbelievably at the unexpected and miraculous appearance of her mother below.

That instant was enough for the Indian Hater. Divining Inocencio's intention, he had pulled back from Shorty beside him, and whipped up his big-bore rifle. It swung high, dropped swiftly and surely to bring the target into the full focus of the telescopic sights. Shorty whirled around. It all happened at once. The high-powered rifle shattering the silence with a tremendous roar. The Indian Hater sprawling on the ground, knocked down by a blow from Shorty's fist. "You Goddamned murderin' bastard! I told you . . ."

What had happened? No one knew. The crowd of men stopped, peering up at the old Indian. Honey, clutching her breast, stared up too. Elsie, also stopped above, was staring transfixed at Inocencio before her.

The old Indian was still braced against the key boulder of the avalanche, legs spread and arms outstretched, but his powerful body seemed curiously and suddenly robbed of strength. His head dropped. The tension went out of his hands and arms. His legs buckled. Slowly, limply, he slid to the ground.

Shorty was still standing above the Indian Hater who was staring upward between the undersheriff's legs with a sardonic grin. Furtively, he patted his rifle. "Never miss, do yeh? Wal, I reckon this pays fer some of them good acres they stole from me!"

In the terrible silence a childish scream rang out, more terrible still. It was the anguished cry of a child for whom the exciting playacting had turned abruptly into stark reality; the scream of a girl confronted with a tragedy she could not comprehend. Unable to move, she still stared transfixed at the limp figure of Inocencio before her. The old Indian lay on his belly, one arm outstretched over a loose pigtail. How humble, harmless and innocent he looked in his dirty shirt, his ragged trousers without a belt, and his worn moccasins. He might have been asleep save for a dark stain spreading, still spreading, over his shirt. Its tragic significance finally broke her spell. She rushed forward, flinging herself down beside him with an agonized wail.

"Inocencio! They've hurt you! Inocencio!"

The old Indian did not move nor speak. Nor did the girl now, her arms wrapped around him.

[137]

Timeless time and fathomless silence were broken for her at last by Honey who, outstripping the men clambering up the slope, rushed upon her. "Elsie! Thank God! Elsie!" She stopped as the girl did not move. Then gently, understandingly, she knelt, pulled the girl back from Inocencio, and wrapped her arms around her.

"Inocencio! Oh, Inocencio!" With a despairing cry, Elsie flung her arms around her mother and broke into gasping sobs.

It was this tableau of mother and child reunited at last that the men saw as they came up the slope. An unkempt woman in ragged dress and torn stockings, her dirty face streaked with tears; and a small girl with one bootless foot, her ludicrous cowboy suit in tatters. Elsie was hugging her mother so tightly they seemed welded together into an immovable cast. Yet over the woman's shoulder she was still staring transfixed at the still body of the old Indian.

"Why did they kill him, Mother? He was good to me. He was the only one who loved me . . . And he wouldn't let that mean man hurt me . . . It was all my fault. I ran away and made him go with me . . . I stole the car . . . " In gasping sobs she let it all out at last.

"Hush, baby. Things just happen. No one knows why. They just do, baby."

Shorty swiftly and mercifully grabbed up a blanket, flung it over Inocencio's body, and stood looking down at it with compassionate pity on his homely face. Elsie lowered her head on Honey's shoulder, comforted by her mother's soothing voice. Around them the posse, fidgeting uneasily in their heavy boots and avoiding each others' eyes, all turned to stare down with somber, accusing looks at the Indian Hater who had remained alone at the bottom of the slope.

The Indian Hater, as if understanding and resenting their silent verdict, flung about and with brutal abandon began lashing his tethered pack of dogs.

It was over, all over at last—the strange and wonderful, terrible and tragic flight from Fiesta that had begun just one week ago on an Indian Summer day under the portal of the *Palácio Real* in Santa Fe. Yet the mystery of this timeless interlude, of this transcendental experience which had been brought to flower and would forever change the lives of its participants, still hung heavy over the little girl. She sat cuddled in her mother's lap, in the back seat of Evans' big car, closing her eyes against its lingering sweetness and its immediate terror.

The sun was beginning to set over the western range. In its red flare the street of El Zaguan was filling with men and cars. At its head, motor running, waited the state police car. The Indian Hater and his dogs were crowded into another; then Evans' and others. Shorty sat in the driver's seat of the station wagon at the rear of the procession. On the floor behind him, where it had been brought on a hastily contrived stretcher, lay the body of Inocencio covered with his faded red blanket. No one spoke; not even in the crowd of villagers lining the road.

There sounded a gentle tap on the partly rolled-down window-pane of Evans' car. Honey looked up to see Dixon standing outside.

"I'm riding back with the state police officers," he said quietly. "I'll be checked out of the hotel by the time you arrive . . . I just wanted to say good-bye, Honey."

"Thank you for seeing us through to the end. I'll remember that, Freddie."

He bowed his head with dignity to Evans and Margaret in the front seat and walked quickly away. Yet the sound of his voice had recalled to Elsie something that seemed far-off and familiar. "Where's Mary?" she asked, opening her eyes and raising her head.

"At home waiting for you. Drawing a hot bath and laying out your favorite dress. The little pink organdie, remember? Then we'll have dinner together, all alone. Just you and Mother."

"So we're going home?"

"Yes, Baby. Home!"

"And what'll we do tomorrow?

"Anything you want to do."

"Buy a napoleon, a chocolate mousse, a new dress—I'm tired of that old organdie! And let's have fun for a change!"

"Anything you want you can have. Always!"

Elsie lay back against her mother's shoulder again, and closed her eyes.

The cars in the procession began to move off, one by one. Shorty, at the end, let out his clutch slowly. The body in the back stirred gently under the faded red blanket. Inocencio, too, was going home.